Luck Of The Draw

By Anna Black

Published By Delphine Publications LLC

© 2010 by Anna Black

ISBN-13: 9780982145579

First Printing April 2010

10 9 8 7 6 5 4 3 2 1

Published and printed in the
United States of America

www.delphinepublications.com

In Loving Memory

Of

Marvin Earl Barnes Sr.

Dad, I know you are not physically here with me to celebrate my accomplishments, but I know you are in heaven celebrating for me. It's because of you I know what it feels like to have a daddy who loved me and I miss you every single day. I love you to pieces, daddy.

Dedication

This book is dedicated to my readers, whom I truly appreciate and I hope that I can make my readers laugh, cry and reflect. I am so excited to release book number two and I hope you guys want to read book three. I am so happy to be able to entertain with words and I am excited that you decided to read Luck of the Draw. This goes to you, my readers; you are the reason to do what I do.

Enjoy!

Acknowledgments

Thank you Lord, thank you Father for blessing me with published book number two. Thanks to my mom, Lue, you are amazing and I hope you are proud. Chris, my husband, my superman, thanks for tons of love and support even when I had doubts that I could go forward. Tyra, mommy wants to give you special thanks for always making me smile on every occasion. You are my sunshine, Tyra. I also want to thank everyone that have supported me and encouraged me because this has not been easy, trust me. I want to say thanks to my true friends, you know who you are. To name names would only reveal those who are not, so I won't. Thanks everyone that supported me with Now You Wanna Come Back, thanks so much for giving my debut book a chance. Thanks Delphine, I am so delighted to be a part of this publication family.

I am grateful to God for so many blessings. To have a creative mind is a gift and I thank Him. To allow my stories to be enjoyed by others is also a blessing. Thank you, my readers, for giving **Luck of the Draw** a chance to be read by you.

Just always remember to "Be You, Do You, & Love You."

Also by Anna Black:

Now You Wanna Come Back

Luck

Of

The

Draw

Chapter One

Kennedy wasn't in the mood for going out that Saturday evening. She had just gotten off from a long day of work at the jewelry store and she was exhausted. Since she owned the store, certain packages that came in could only be verified by her, so that day had her mentally and physically tired. She drove home telling herself, 'I can't wait to put my feet up and sip on a glass of something that will help me to relax.'

She walked in the door, leaving everything she carried into the house in the foyer and told herself that she'd get it later. She climbed the steps to her bedroom with a smile on her face because she finally reached her destination to a peaceful place, but her best friend Cherae was at her door within minutes, pressing her to go out with them to the club. She took off her shoes trying to ignore Cherae as she took off her clothes and then she slipped into her comfy robe.

"Come on girl, all you need is a shower and you'll be refreshed. Teresa said she'll be here by 11:30 and that will give you plenty of time to get some rest and be ready. You work at a jewelry store Kay, not on a farm, so you can't be that tired," she whined.

Kennedy knew that she was in for a battle if Teresa was also there in her ear to go out. She knew that would be a no win situation. They always cornered her and talked her into going out with them, even when she really didn't want to go. The thing was; they'd drink more than she and they knew she'd be sober enough to drive their drunken behinds home, so she knew they just wanted to get their drink on.

"Okay man damn. I will go, but don't think I'm driving because after the day I just had, I want to get some liquor in me and I'm not driving you drunk heifers home this time. I'm the one who's going to be in the back seat passed out, understood?"

"Yes, yes," Cherae said with excitement.

"Now get out of here so I can rest my nerves before Ree gets here," Kennedy playfully ordered.

"No problem madam. I will let you be, but you know I'm gon' be right back up here to make sure you are getting ready. And can I borrow your little blue Donna Karen purse? I need it for tonight," she asked.

Kennedy wanted to say no because Cherae always borrowed her things, but she was too sweet to say no and it wasn't like she was going to need it.

"Yea, it's in the closet on the bottom rack and when you come back up to so-call check on me, you better have me a glass of wine in your hand too," Kennedy said with a smile.

Cherae was her girl no matter what and she loved her to death. She did a lot for Cherae and it didn't bother her one bit. She just wondered when Cherae was going to get herself together and stop being so needy. She was so dependant and Kennedy didn't understand how she settled when she had so much opportunity to be so much better. She had no kids or excuses to hold her back from doing something with her life and she wasn't paying Kennedy a dime to live there. Cherae just thought her looks would land her a rich man and after almost thirty-four years of trying to land a millionaire, she was still unlucky to accomplish that mission.

Kennedy walked into her massive walk-in closet and it didn't take long for her to find something to wear. She had so many clothes, shoes, purses and hats; she didn't have to go through a million and one channels to look fabulous. Kennedy was a plump woman, full-figured society would say, but at a size sixteen, there was nothing bad anyone could say about her. She was conservative in some ways, but she knew how to turn on the sexy.

She loved going out with her girlfriends and even though she was the heavier sister, she still turned a few heads when they went out together. She knew she was gorgeous because her daddy taught her that. She never felt more or less beautiful than her two girls, and she did know for a fact that they all had it going on.

Teresa was an averaged size woman, not fat at all Kennedy thought to herself when she'd hear her complaining about how she gained a pound or two. Teresa stood about five feet and at one hundred and thirty pounds, she looked good in everything she wore because she was curvy. Her hips and ass filled her jeans to a tee, but her B cupped breast couldn't go without a padded bra. She had pretty light brown skin and it was smooth and clear. Her short and sassy hair style would always receive compliments from women and men and it looked good on her round face.

As pretty as Kennedy thought Teresa was, she hardly understood how she always had man trouble. Kennedy realized, after meeting and getting to know Teresa that looks had absolutely nothing to do with getting a man because Teresa's bright smile and gorgeous figure didn't make a man stay with her and most of her men turned out to be crazy.

Then there was Cherae, the bombshell of the trio; the head turner, the show stopper. She knew she looked good and didn't try to front like she wasn't the bomb. She's high yellow with long, straight, dark hair that she keeps highlighted blonde. Women would swear she wears a weave, but it's all hers. Her body is tight because she works out five days a week to maintain her size four frame. Her eyes are hazel naturally, but most people think they are fake. She has a pear shaped face, with a little cute nose and since she never knew her dad, Kennedy would sometimes joke that her daddy was of another race because her momma is Kennedy's complexion and has a big nose. Cher stands at five feet two inches and although she is slim, her body is shaped perfect with a C cupped breast size that could go easily without a bra for support and she never looks like a skinny girl in her jeans.

Cherae doesn't have relationship issues and getting a man has never been one of her downfalls, meeting a man with a lot of money is what caused her problems. She had plenty of marriage proposals and dated numerous men, but she just doesn't have it upstairs. She is just a beauty with no brains, looking for a free ride.

Of Kennedy's two friends, Teresa has all the good qualities of a woman, including a sweet personality. She is always honest and tries to always be straight up with folks. She never acts like she was better than others and most of all, she is fair. She is the cool head of the group and wouldn't argue with anyone over anything at anytime. She and Kennedy are close and spend more time together because they work together. They met about six years ago when Kennedy took over one of her dad's jewelry stores.

Teresa had no experience nor did she know anything about the jewelry business, but she was the only person that Kennedy liked when she interviewed. She and Kennedy hit it off and realized that they had a lot in common, except for the knowledge of diamonds, silver and gold. So, after she promised Kennedy she would learn the business, Kennedy hired her and was so glad she did.

Cherae on the other hand, was a different case. She and Kennedy has been friends their entire lives and for so long Kennedy has told her that she was not going to be able to live off her good looks, but Cherae being as irresistible as she thinks she is, had men paying her way for everything. She used men to her advantage, but got caught up on a wealthy, older gentleman that put her up in a nice condo downtown. He was married but that didn't mean a thing to Cher because he was very rich and had his own company and as long as Cher took trips with him and filled in as his woman when he wanted a show piece on his arm, he took care of her. That lasted a couple years 'til he found a younger superstar to cater to and he dropped her ass and she had to move in with Kennedy.

Kennedy wasn't so torn up about it because she loved Cherae like a sister. She was an only child and she and Cherae were practically raised together, being that they met in the second grade. When they graduated high school they parted briefly, because after the first year of college away from home, Kennedy was home sick and she went back home to attend school near her family, so she and Cherae were right back together. Once Kennedy got her Masters, her daddy decided it was time for her to take over the store that he ran and owned for twenty-four years. Kennedy was honored to take over and have her own store because her two cousins ran two other locations that belonged to her uncles, Kendal and Keith.

They were a close knit family and accepted Cher as family until Cher dated Kennedy's cousin Kory for a while and showed her natural simple ass. The family viewed her a little different, yet still respected her because she and Kennedy were so close. They were like "two peas in a pod," Kennedy's daddy Kenneth would say and told his nephews for Kennedy's sake to grin and bear her. Kennedy knew they didn't care for her much after the break up, but she figured she messed over Kory like she did all men because that was the norm for Cher. She warned Kory how Cher was prior, but no he just had to have her and she tried to drain his pockets. Kennedy tried to stay out of their relationship and not take sides, but they always involved her, so she was not sad when they finally broke up.

Chapter Two

Kennedy went into her bathroom and started the shower. She pulled her hair back and washed the make-up from her day away from her face. She leaned closer to the mirror to inspect her skin and smiled at her pretty, smooth complexion. She was medium brown toned and she thanked God that she had never encountered any acne problems. Her round face and pretty eyes didn't need a lot of make up in the mornings. She was good as long as her hair was relaxed and eyebrows were arched. Her hair was a little longer than shoulder length, but she loved to wear it curly most of the time for convenience. She only wore pressed power and lip gloss because she was blessed with a beautiful smile. Her daddy spent a lot of money at the orthodontist to make sure her teeth were perfect and it showed.

She went back into her room, turned on her system and pressed the button 'til she landed on Ne-Yo's new CD. She was looking for Jennifer Hudson's new CD, but she was too impatient to wait for the changer to land on the right disk. She got into the shower and the hot water was refreshing to her skin. She took her time in the shower because it felt good and the water was nice and hot. She shaved her legs and under arms and it refreshed her. When she got out, she put on her robe and went downstairs to pour herself a glass of wine. She was revitalized and ready to do the damn thing. Her whole attitude about going out had changed and she couldn't wait to get the party started.

"Cher what time are you trying to leave?" she yelled from the kitchen.

Cherae came into the kitchen half dressed as usual and

Kennedy just over looked her. Since Cherae had the body of an aerobics instructor she rarely covered up. She was always in something skimpy or barely anything at all.

"Well I guess around 11:30 when Ree gets here. Can you manage to be ready by then Ms. Kennedy?" she asked because Kennedy was usually slow about getting ready.

"Yeah girl, it's what, 8:17?" she said, looking at the clock on the stove and answering her own question. "I am refreshed now baby and I'm gon' be ready before you."

"Yea you say that, but I know you Kay," she said, grabbing Kennedy's glass and taking a swallow of her wine.

"What? Girl, please. I'm going to be ready this time. I already know what I'm wearing, so yes I'll be ready," she said, taking her glass.

"Well when you hear the doorbell you know your time is up."

"Yea I know, now move yo' half naked ass outta my way," Kennedy said and headed for the stairs.

"Girl you know I can't stand wearing clothes, especially after a hot shower," Cherae said, pouring herself a glass of wine.

"Yea that's the excuse you use to stay naked."

"Shut up," she said and they laughed.

Kennedy went back upstairs, sat in her chair and put her feet up. She grabbed her novel from her little table that she had sitting aside her chair and put her glass down. She was at the end of her book *"Who Can I Run To,"* by Anna Black, so she figured she'd go ahead and finish it to kill a little time.

Although she didn't want it to come to an end, she was about three or four chapters away. She tried to start reading, but she stopped because she started to feel sleepy all over again, so she got up and decided she'd go ahead and flat iron her hair. That was a better idea anyway, that way she would definitely be ready on time. The CD changer finally changed to Jennifer Hudson and Kennedy was just about done getting ready. She was standing in the mirror doing her face when Teresa walked in.

"Girl, no you're not ready, it's a miracle," she joked.

"Oh yes I am baby. Now what?" she joked back with her.

"Something good gon' happen tonight if you are ready.

Chile, you are the slowest woman I've ever met in my life."

"Well tonight I'm ready and I hope you are prepared to drive because I'm about to get my groove on," she said, dancing in the mirror.

"Aw, watch out now," Teresa said, coming into the bathroom and they shared the mirror.

Teresa was already completely dressed, but she had a habit of going through Kennedy's make-up and enhancing her face a little more because Kennedy had the good stuff in a variety of colors.

"Ya'll slow poke's ready?" Cherae asked, coming into the bathroom too.

"Yeah, we're ready and where are the rest of your clothes, Ms. Thang?" Kennedy asked.

"What, do you think this is too sexy?" Cherae asked like she was totally clueless.

"Um yea, I can damn near see your nipples Cher. How many times do I have to tell you, you are beautiful as ever, you don't have to dress like that to get attention. Men would fall all over you if you had on a turtle neck and snow pants."

"Yeah Cher, you are gorgeous and that outfit is like a couple of pieces of material, barely hanging on," Teresa added.

"Come on y'all, I've been waiting all winter to be able to wear this and now that it's finally warm enough to wear it, I wanna wear it," she said, turning to the side admiring herself. She thought she looked good in that outfit and the middle of May had finally come to allow her to wear it.

"Whatever Cher. It is no use, you gon' do yo' thang. Ain't no stopping you from being you."

"That's right, now chop, chop," Cherae said, clapping her hands and walking out. Teresa and Kennedy just looked at each other.

"That's yo' friend," Teresa said.

"I know, but you gotta love her," Kennedy said and blotted her lips.

They managed to convince Cherae to put on a different outfit and she came out with a little skimpy red dress that they didn't think was a good choice either, but it was better than the last outfit.

They got to the club and it wasn't that crowded, but they still were unlucky getting a good table so they decided to sit at one of the bars in the back. Tony was the hook up bartender and since the music wasn't as loud back there, they could hear each other speak.

After about an hour or so, the club was packed and they were enjoying themselves. They ordered another round and sat there and talked and laughed. The music was on point and Cherae turned around to scan the room to see who she wanted to lure over to ask her to dance. Kennedy and Teresa were both shocked when she turned down the last fifteen dudes that approached her.

"Damn, where are the fine brotha's at tonight?" Cher asked. Kennedy and Teresa turned around to scan the room with her and it was like they all spotted him at the same time.

"Oh no baby, that right there," Kennedy tried to say.

"Oh baby you ain't even looking…at that… brotha right there," Teresa said, cutting Kennedy off.

"I already know," Cherae added.

"No, no, no, baby, I saw him first," Teresa said.

"Girl stop lying, I saw him first," Kennedy said.

"It doesn't matter, because that brother is going home with me tonight," Cherae said.

"Wait, wait, wait, y'all know the rules," Kennedy said.

"Kay damn, you know I saw him first," Cherae spat.

"How you gon' trip Cherae? As soon as I turned around I saw him," Teresa said.

"Oh my God, he is coming this way," Kennedy said.

"Well this is where it gets easy," Cherae said, sitting up tall on her stool. She already knew he would come over and choose her.

"Ooohhh, you get on my nerves," Kennedy said to Cherae and then he was standing between them before Cherae could say something back.

"Excuse me ladies," he said, reaching past them. "Hey, Tony, let me get a double Crown with a splash of Coke on the rocks."

"Gotcha," Tony said and then went to fix the drink.

Cherae was looking at him like he was meat on the grill and Kennedy knew not to stare, so she just checked out his reflection in the mirror behind the bar.

"How are you ladies tonight?" he asked, looking at Kennedy.

"Oh we are good, Mr...," Cherae answered, extending her little hand.

"Roberson, Julian Roberson," he answered, shaking her hand. "And you are?"

"Cherae, but my friends call me Cher."

"Well Cherae, nice to meet you," he said and Tony came with his drink. "Thanks man and whatever these ladies are drinking, give them a round. You ladies enjoy," he said and walked away.

"Damn, damn, damn he fine," Cherae said.

"Girl you ain't got to tell me," Teresa said, agreeing.

"Oh yes and guess what?" Kennedy asked with a smirk.

"What?" Cher asked.

"He didn't fall at'cha feet Cher, that is a new one," she said and she and Teresa laughed.

"Well my dear, he bought us a round of drinks didn't he? My babies are good for something," she said, lifting her breast a little.

"Yea, air bags," Teresa joked.

"Ha, ha, ha," Cher said with attitude.

"Well first of all Miss Thang, he didn't hit on you, so that means what?" Teresa asked.

"What?" Cherae asked.

"Well Cher, space girl that means he is still free game and we have to play by the rules."

"Yea, yea, yea, I know," she said, disappointed.

"So ladies, are y'all ready?" Teresa asked.

"Do we have a choice?" Cherae asked with attitude.

"If you want to remain friends after this," Kennedy said.

"Alright, alright," Cherae whined.

They all pulled out their business cards. They folded them in half and put them on the counter. They called Tony over and asked him to pick a card. They all sat there and watched closely as he picked up the card that said Kennedy R. Banks and Kennedy almost jumped off her stool.

"Damn man, why you choose that one?" Cherae barked.

"Sorry baby, I didn't know you wanted me to pick yours," he said and winked.

"Yea, yea, whatever man," Cherae said and was mad. "Gon' on, go get'em, tiger."

"You know the rules. We fold our cards, lay them in a line and whichever the bartender or server draws is the one who wins," Teresa said.

"Yeah, I know. Now if y'all would excuse me, I need to go work the room," Cher said, coming off of her stool.

"You're not going to go over there with me Cher?"

"Hell no, you won the draw, now do yo' thang girl," she said and walked away.

"Hater," Kennedy said. "Come on Ree, go over with me."

"Where did he go?" Teresa asked.

"He's over there at that table in the corner."

"Damn girl, you got good eyes. I see why you know diamonds."

"Come on Ree," Kennedy said, almost pulling her off the stool.

"Okay, okay," she said and they walked over to his table.

He was doing what looked to them, like some type of paperwork and they thought that was odd with him being in a crowded club.

"Um, hi…, Julian right?"

"Yes," he said and smiled.

"Hi, I'm Kennedy and this is my girlfriend Teresa and we just wanted to say thanks for the drinks."

"Oh no problem ladies, it was my pleasure," he said. They stood there feeling uncomfortable.

"Yeah thank you Julian, but if y'all would excuse me, I have to go to the ladies room," Teresa said.

Kennedy wanted to slap her. She hadn't been with her a minute and she was bailing. Kennedy was left standing there feeling awkward.

"Well again, thanks Julian, that was sweet," she said and

was about to walk away.

"Kennedy," he called out.

"Yea," she said, turning back to him.

"Listen, I am the new owner of this club. Tell me, do you come here a lot?" he asked. She stood there gazing for a moment. Kennedy was mesmerized by his medium brown shaded skin and sexy eyes.

"Yea, I come here quite a bit. It's about the only spot that we have a good time at. I always say to my girls I wish it was more options in this town," she said nervously. There were plenty of hot spots in Chicago, but they didn't want to drive too far to party.

"I was just wondering. You know how it goes, word gets out that there is new management or new ownership, people panic..., think that things will change, so I was just curious what you think about this place," he said.

"It's cool, but I think it is a tragedy to see a man sitting in the corner doing paperwork. I mean, that is a sign that someone is not here to party," she said and they laughed.

"You know what, you are right," he said and smiled. Kennedy thought it was the sexiest smile she'd ever seen on a man. He looked at her standing and offered her a seat and she quickly accepted. "I would be in my office but I had it painted today and the fumes were killing me."

"Well you might want to observe tonight and save the paperwork 'til tomorrow or 'til you close, because it's party time, not paperwork time," she joked and he laughed again.

"Well I guess you are right again," he said, taking his briefcase from the floor beside him. He put his paperwork away and the waitress came over.

"Would you like anything, Mr. Roberson?"

"Yea, give me a Crown and Coke. And you?" he asked Kennedy.

"Oh, Chardonnay please," she said and the waitress didn't hesitate to get their drinks.

"So, what do you do Kennedy?" he asked and she couldn't help but stare and then finally answered.

"Well I am a jeweler. You may have heard of my company, KBanks Jewelers."

"Yea, I saw a store near the mall."

"Yea, that's my location."

"Okay."

"Do you wear jewelry Julian?"

"No..., not too much. Watches are my thing, but all the other stuff, not too much. I'm not flashy," he said and they chuckled.

"Well believe it or not, I'm not big on jewelry either, but diamonds have been the topic of my life. My great grandfather started the business and then my granddaddy and of course my daddy and two uncles. My daddy was the only one to have a girl, so now I'm the first female descendant to take the throne," she said proudly with a bright smile that he thought was beautiful.

"Wow," he said, returning a sexy smile, Kennedy thought to herself. She didn't know what his story was, but she knew he was fine as hell.

"Yeah, I know, right?" she said.

They continued an endless conversation. Kennedy kept looking around for her friends but she couldn't locate either one of them. After the DJ called last call, she and Julian wondered where all of the time went. She looked at her watch and was shocked it was so late.

"Wow man, it's late," he said, glancing at the time on his watch.

"Yeah, I know right? Where are my friends?" Kennedy asked, still trying to spot one of them. She finally saw Teresa talking to a guy and it seemed as if she was enjoying what he was saying because she was smiling and looking at the brother like she wanted to eat him alive. She still hadn't located Cherae, but she figured she would find her soon.

"Well if you need me to, I can get you home."

"No I'm good, my girls wouldn't leave me."

"I know, but if you wanted me to give you a lift, I can," he said. She could tell he wanted to continue to hang with her.

"Okay, let me let my girl know and I'll be right back."

"I got to run up to my office for a couple of things and I'll be right back," he said, giving her a warm smile.

"Okay well, I'll see you in a moment."

"Okay," he said and she walked over to Teresa.

"Ree, where is Cher?"

"Girl I dunno, she probably left with that guy I saw her talking to earlier."

"No, she wouldn't just leave without telling us."

"Oh yeah?" Teresa said, nodding at the door. Cher was walking out in arms with a fine brother that looked like he was a pro basketball player because he was tall."

"Oh no she didn't," Kennedy said, watching her walk out the door.

"That's yo' friend," Teresa said again, something she always said.

"Whatever, anyway, Julian is going to give me a ride home. Are you okay with that?"

"Yea baby, I'm fine."

"Are you sure, because I can tell him no."

"Kay please, I'm good. Go on, just call me when you get in."

"Okay girl, be safe," Kennedy said and kissed her cheek. She walked away and went back over to the table to wait for Julian.

Chapter Three

The next morning, the sun was bright and Kennedy was trying to block out the light. She put her pillow over her head, but the heat was too much for her to bear so she moved the pillow and pulled the comforter over her head. After a couple of minutes, it was hot underneath her covers too. She finally gave up and got up. As soon as she sat up, her head reminded her of all the drinks she had the night before. She paused for a second or two before getting up and smiled to herself when she glanced at the card that was on her nightstand.

When Julian dropped her off at her place, he gave her his card and told her to give him a call when she had time. She picked up the card and stared at it for a few moments before she finally went to the bathroom. When she went downstairs the house was empty and quiet. She immediately knew that Cherae hadn't come home and was sure she went home with the guy she saw her leave the club with. Kennedy shook her head, but didn't think anything of it because Cherae was a grown ass woman and was entitled to do whatever she wanted to do, with whomever she chose.

Kennedy opened the front door, got the paper and went into the kitchen to make herself a little breakfast. She loved her kitchen because it had the original woods floors the house was built with. Her home was over fifty years old, but after the extensive renovations, it was modern and her huge gourmet kitchen had top of the line appliances and granite countertops. She wished she did more cooking in it, but since it was just her and Cher, they rarely prepared meals other than breakfast on the weekends. She sat in her window seat and was happy about spring finally being there because in the winter, the chill was too cold for her to enjoy her window seat without a blanket.

After eating and reading the paper, she cleared the table and loaded the dishwasher. She was about to head up the stairs to her master suite, but she heard the door and knew it was Cherae coming in, so she stopped, sat on the steps and waited for her to come inside so they could chat a little. She was curious about her night and she wasn't expecting to get attitude from her.

"Hey girl, how was your night? I saw you leaving with that tall, fine ass guy," Kennedy said to Cherae.

"Yea, he was fine. No biggie," she said nonchalantly because she wished it would have been Julian she left the club with.

She had a major attitude the night before. Every time she glanced over at him and Kennedy smiling and carrying on what looked like good conversation pissed her off. How could he choose Kennedy over her she wondered, pissed at that idea. She hoped they hadn't gotten together the night before because if she saw him again, she was going to approach him.

"Well it must have been a biggie, you stayed out with him all night."

"Oh so you're my mother now?" she asked with attitude.

"No and what is your problem? Is everything okay?" Kennedy asked with concern.

"I'm fine," Cherae said and then went into the bathroom down the hall by her bedroom.

"Well you don't seem fine Cher. What's wrong?" Kennedy asked, following her to the bathroom. She stood at the door and waited for Cher to answer, but she brushed by her. Kennedy followed her into her room. "Cherae Monique, what's going on?" she asked again.

"Nothing Kay, damn. Why are things so dramatic with you?"

"It's not Cher, I was just asking. You seem upset, like something is wrong and I am just making sure you are okay," she said, wondering why Cherae was acting so childish when she was only trying to help.

"Well I'm fine okay? And the tall dude was fine yes and he

has it going on, but the brotha can't fuck," she said, taking off her clothes.

"Cher..., you didn't?" Kennedy asked, but was not surprised. Cherae had gone home plenty of times with guys she met at the club and Kennedy knew they were not leaving just to talk.

"Didn't what? Come on now Kay, don't play me. You know how I do," she said so casually.

"But Cher..., I just...," she said and decided not to lecture her again. "You know what, never mind," she said.

"Yeah, that's what I thought," Cherae said, giving more attitude. Kennedy knew to just leave her alone.

"Okay, well I'll be in my room if you need me," she said, walking away.

"Yea okay," she said.

Kennedy didn't know what Cherae's problem was, but she didn't have the energy to deal with her. When she got upstairs, she climbed back into her king sized bed and grabbed the remote. She propped a couple pillows behind her, making sure it was one directly behind her head because her headboard was upholstered in a neutral bone colored material that had the look of suede. Her walls were a warm shade of brown and her other pieces were marble. Her chair and ottoman were upholstered in the exact same material as her headboard and even though it was heavily scotched guarded like her chair and ottoman, she was always cautious because of the oils in her hair.

She flipped through the channels of her thirty two inch plasma and muted the volume when she couldn't find anything interesting to watch. She reached for her novel to finish it, noticed Julian's card and fought the urge to call him. She hated she didn't give him her number instead, because now she had to be the initiator and that was totally uncomfortable for her. She hadn't been in any serious relationships due to fear of being hurt. Her dad constantly warned her about men and how evil they could be to women, so she guarded her heart, afraid to give it to a man. She had flings and actually kicked it with one guy named Travis for a little over two and a half years 'til she felt like she was catching feelings, so she backed off.

She wanted love; yes. dreamt of having a good relationship, but when was it going to happen and with whom was something Kennedy didn't give much thought to. She had everything; family, friends, a great career doing what she loved to do and quite a bit of money. Romance was way on the bottom of her list of things to do, so she didn't know why she kept smiling when she thought of Julian. She turned his card down, grabbed her book and finished reading her last three or four chapters.

After a couple of hours of the television watching her, she got up. She powered off the television and closed the marble doors of her armoire that housed her plasma. She knew if she was going to be successful in not calling Julian she was going to have to make herself busy and that was her game plan. She showered and pulled her hair back into a ponytail. She looked at her reflection and thought about cutting her hair, to try something new. She wondered what it would look like to have a short style and how would she maintain it.

Her momma had long hair and when she got sick with cancer and lost her hair, her daddy would always say, "Kay-Kay, never ever cut your hair. A woman's hair is her glory," and that's what had kept her from cutting her hair.

Her momma died when she was a freshman in high school and when she passed, her daddy paid Miss Lucille, a lady from the church, to do her hair every week. He would threaten Miss Lucille by telling her, "If you trim my baby's hair more than the average trim on the ends, there will be hell to pay." Although that was a little excessive, Kennedy understood because she thought that her mom was more devastated with losing her hair than fighting cancer.

She remembered her momma sobbing because she had to wear wigs and how she began to not enjoy her own reflection in the mirror because her hair was everything to her. It was so long, healthy and pretty and she always kept it fixed really nice. Kennedy was just about to let her memories of her momma bring her down, but then she heard a tap on her door. She knew it could only be one person, so she said, "Come in."

"Listen Kay, I'm sorry about downstairs. I didn't mean to snap at you like that," Cherae said.

"It's cool Cher, I'm not trippin', but what's wrong?" Kennedy asked.

"Well you know I gotta pay my car note on Tuesday, right? And Gregory was supposed to break me off the payment, but he is trippin' and I don't have it."

"See, I keep telling you to stop depending on these guys to pay your bills. Every time you are kicking it with a man, you expect them to be paying your bills and you have to stop doing that."

"I know Kay, but what happened was, I wanted to buy these shoes and this outfit the other day and I asked Greg to get it for me and he told me he would, but when he was supposed to meet me at the mall he couldn't make it and he told me to go ahead and get what I wanted and he'd get it back to me. I told him that I was spending my car payment and he promised, but now he won't answer my calls and Tuesday is right around the corner," she whined.

"Look Cher, as much as I want to fuss and cuss, I know it won't do any good because I've been telling you for years the same ole thing. I will give you the money and if Gregory gives you the money, I want my money back. I can't keep bailing you out, Cher. I can't keep doing this," Kennedy said, trying not to fuss.

"Thank you Kay and I'll pay you back. I promise."

"No you won't, you always say you will, but you never do. How much do you need?"

"Three-hundred, I have the rest and if he gives it to me I will give it back."

"Well I'm going to go out for a while and I'll stop by the cash station and give it to you when I get back."

"Thank you Kay, you are a lifesaver," she said, then stood to leave but stopped. "Oh, how did it go with Julian?"

"It was cool, we talked and he drove me home," Kennedy said like no big deal.

"He drove you home? So, did he come in?"

"No, he just dropped me off."

"Kay come on, that's it?"

"Yes why? I don't know him like that Cher," she said, frowning.

"Don't be frowning up your face like that. You know what I mean Kay, not like I'm saying you should have slept with him. I'm just asking. You are so slow," she said, shaking her head.

"No, you are just fast," she commented.

"Well all I know is, if it hadda been me, he would still be here right now."

"Well I guess that's you, but I don't know anything about that man. He just bought the club and he could have a lady or kids, shit…, we didn't talk that long."

"Girl I saw you over at that table with him talking all night, now come on. Y'all had to have talked about something," she said, trying to see if he was still available.

"Yeah work and the club and that's about it. We didn't touch on anything too personal."

"So are you gonna see him again?"

"Maybe, he gave me a card and I have his number, so we'll see."

"Well you won the draw and you'd be a fool to sleep on that," Cher said and sashayed out the door. She had on the smallest shorts that she could find with a cut off wife beater.

"Well I'll keep that in mind, Miss Thang," Kennedy said as she shut her door behind Cher.

'That chile needs prayer,' Kennedy thought to herself as she grabbed her purse. She didn't know where she would be going, but she had to go somewhere to not think about calling Julian. She grabbed her cell phone, her keys and purposely left his card on her nightstand. She walked down the steps and wondered if she should invite Cher out with her on her trip to nowhere and she decided not to.

She got into her Denali, headed down the street and decided she'd go by the bookstore to get a book or two. She got three new books and stopped by the grocery store and picked up a few items. She got home and she was happy to see Cher was gone. It was still early and she didn't have much to do, so she decided to clean a little bit. Once she finished dusting and swifting her wood floors and changing her sheets, it was still early, not even seven. She grabbed a book by Tamika Newhouse called *'The Ultimate No No,'* from her bag and sat in her comfy chair and rested her feet on her ottoman.

She looked around her room before opening her book and was pleased with the way it looked. Her home was a fixer upper and her daddy thought she was crazy for not wanting a brand new house, but her being his only child and spoiled as she was, he let her buy it and hired the best contracting company in Chicago to do it exactly like she wanted it. It took two years to get it perfect and not even six months after the renovation, Cher moved in.

It wasn't so bad living with Cher because for one, Cher was a clean woman and kept things nice, just the way Kennedy liked it. She wasn't one of those type of women that you saw looking good in the streets, but kept a nasty house. She was neat and tidy and took care of the house just as well as Kennedy did, so they got along. The only thing Kennedy hated was the men in and out of her house. Cher would have a date with a different man every night. Kennedy was so glad her room was on the main floor because even upstairs, she could hear Cher screaming and moaning like a professional porn star and Kennedy knew if she was on the same floor with her things would have not been good. She may have put her out a long time ago.

Cher and Kennedy, for the most part shared their living space well. After a while, Cher complied with Kennedy's request to stop bringing so many strange men into her home. She slowed down a lot, but not completely. There were times when Kennedy would come home and not only did Cher have a date over, her date would have a friend with him and Cher would expect Kennedy to entertain her date's friend while she entertained her date, no matter how late it was and that shit had to cease immediately.

One night, she pulled that move and took her date into her bedroom. It was after two in the morning, leaving Kennedy to entertain her date's friend. Kennedy had to put him out because he just assumed she'd take him upstairs and sing the same tune Cher was singing from her room. Kennedy was so mad at Cher; she told her if she did that shit again she'd have to go. Since then, Cher knew not to invite blind dates for Kennedy because she didn't want to be hooked up, especially not with a man that had anything to do with Cher.

A couple hours went by and it was finally after seven.

Kennedy was proud that she didn't call Julian and hoped she'd make it through the entire week without calling him. Although she thought a lot about him, she didn't want to seem too eager. *'Damn, girl, why didn't you just give him your card after he gave you his?'* She asked herself as she walked down the stairs.

She went into the kitchen and looked in the fridge, wondering what she would eat for dinner. She wasn't too hungry, but she knew she had to eat something. She grabbed the cranberry juice and just as she reached for a glass, she heard Cher coming in the front door and she was not alone. She was with the tall gentleman from the night before, who Kennedy remembered her saying was not good in bed.

"Hey Kay, what's up? This is Cortez. Cortez, this is my roomy and best friend Kennedy," Char said, introducing them.

"Hello Kennedy," he said, extending his hand and they shook.

"Hi Cortez, it's nice to meet you."

"Likewise," he said and smiled.

'My God, he is gorgeous,' Kennedy thought as she admired his smile. All of a sudden, she wished Julian was there too. Cher wouldn't be the only one entertaining a fine man.

"Would you like something to drink?" Cher asked Cortez.

"Sure," he said, standing near the kitchen island.

"You can have a seat," Kennedy offered him.

"Thanks," he said and pulled out one of the stools and sat at the island.

"Would you like liquor or wine?" Cher asked.

"Well actually, some juice or water will be fine. I have an early day tomorrow, so I don't need a drink."

"Suit yourself," she said and poured him a glass of the cranberry juice that was out on the counter. She opened the wine cooler, grabbed a bottle and got the corkscrew to open it while he and Kennedy got acquainted.

"So, what do you do Cortez?" Kennedy asked, making conversation. She was still searching for something to eat.

"Well I am in real estate. Business has been good, so I have to go in a little early tomorrow if I'm going to make all of my appointments.

"Oh, I see."

"You have a lovely home Cher."

"Thank you," Cherae and Kennedy said at the same time. Kennedy looked at her. Not that she was trying to embarrass Cher, but that was her home and she put a lot of blood, sweat and tears into her home and Cher had no part in that. "Thank you," Kennedy said, speaking up. "It was a fixer upper and I can show you the pictures of how awful it was before all of the renovations."

"Really?" he asked, surprised.

Cherae poured her wine into her glass while rolling her eyes. She sat the bottle down and gave him the glass of juice before she put the wine away. Kennedy reached and handed him a coaster to set it on.

"Yes, everything here is damn near new. Except for the floors, the wood is original, we just sanded and stained them," she said, finally giving up on her quest for food. She grabbed some grapes instead and went to the sink to rinse them.

"Well Kennedy, I'd love to see those before pictures, but it looks amazing now," he said and sipped his juice.

Cher stood close to him and tried to not show the irritation on her face about Kennedy correcting her about the house. She knew it wasn't her home, but Kennedy didn't have to make her look like that in front of Cortez.

"So, Cortez why don't you follow me into the living room," she said, not inviting Kennedy. Kennedy was fine with that. She had, after all just gone down to get something to eat.

"Well it was nice meeting you, Kennedy."

"You too Cortez," she said. He got up and followed Cherae into the living room.

Kennedy grabbed her grapes and cranberry juice and went back to her room. After she finished, she took a shower and put on her bed clothes. It was around 9:15 and she decided she might as well call it a night. She got in the bed and turned off the television. She switched on her lamp and there was the card again. It was still lying faced down, but looking at her from the nightstand.

She ignored it again and grabbed her novel to pick up where she left off. A few minutes later, she heard the porn star again. She grabbed the remote to her system and hit the volume 'til she was able to drown out the moans and groans of her best friend. She shook her head and thought to herself, *'For Cortez not to be so great in bed, Cher is putting on one hell of a performance.'*

It was close to 10:30 and she was sleepy. She put her book down and lowered the volume of the music. She was relieved to hear silence and figured they were done. She took one last glance at the card and turned out the light. She didn't have to force herself into her deep night of good sleep.

Chapter Four

"Hey, what's going on?" Teresa asked when Kennedy walked in. She made it in that morning a little earlier than Kennedy, so she decided to start setting up.

"Nothing too much, how are you?" Kennedy said, surprised to see her in already. "You're here early."

"Girl, I was so excited. I woke up bright and early and I'm feeling good," she said, smiling.

"Damn, you must be the way you are smiling," Kennedy said, keying in the code to open the locked door to get on the other side of the counter.

"Well let me tell you why I'm smiling," she said, stopping what she was doing. She was smiling like she hit the lottery and Kennedy was dying to hear her good news. "Do you remember that guy I was talking to Saturday night?"

"Yea, I remember. The dude you were talking to right before I left?"

"Yes him, well we exchanged numbers and girl we went out last night. Kay, this man is the bomb! You hear me? He was so sweet and I had such a good time with him and I plan to see him again," she said excited.

Kennedy couldn't believe she gave it up too. "Aw, not you too," Kennedy said, putting her purse and keys down on the floor behind the counter. She normally took her things straight to her office, but this she had to hear.

"Not me too what?" Teresa asked, confused. They only went out to dinner the night before and they had a good time. She wondered what Kennedy was talking about.

"Gave up the goods like Cher. That guy she left with, his name is Cortez and she gave him some Saturday night and said it was whack and then last night she brings him home and I hear her giving him some again."

"No ma'am, hold on. I said we went out. I had a good time, but I didn't give him any. It wasn't nothing like that honey."

"Oh, okay. I was just curious," she said, happy that Teresa had some type of self control.

"Hold on now, I'm not knocking Cher because hey, she can do whomever she pleases and I'm not gon' act like I have never given a man any on the first night, but hell, that was back when I was stuck on stupid. I'm too old to be going out like that. I am not young and crazy like I used to be. That shit got old, trust me," she said, putting her hand on her hip, looking at Kennedy like *'you got the wrong one.'*

"Well Cher doesn't think she is ever going to get old."

"She can believe that if she wants to, but anyway, back to my friend. Oh my God Kay he is thirty six, divorced and has an eleven year old son that lives with him. He is a contractor and he is eligible," she said, bursting with excitement.

Kennedy thought she may want to slow it down and not get so excited. "Okay…," she said, waiting for more.

"Okay…, okay, that means that he could be potential. And, we had a good time last night and we are going out again tonight."

"Okay Ree, but don't get too excited," she said, not enthused.

"Why not?"

"Because you said the same thing about Lorenz and…," she said.

"And you know what? You didn't even have to go there Kay. That man was crazy," she said and then they laughed.

"I know he was, but you was all geeked up like you are now and what happened?" she said, taking her back to reality.

"Okay, okay, bubble buster, but if he is the one, even if it's five or ten years from now, you will be my Maid of Honor, right?"

"And you know it," she said and then they hugged.

"So what is up with you and Julian?"

"Nothing," Kennedy said imperturbably.

"What do you mean nothing? What happened when he drove you home on Saturday night?" Teresa asked as she moved about the store putting merchandise in the glass cases. She wanted to know her juicy story too.

"Nothing, he gave me a card and that was it."

"You're kidding right?"

"No, I'm not kidding."

"First of all Kay, you've never left the club with a man since we've been friends. For once would you loosen up and take some risk and let go. I mean, live a little."

"Risk on what? What was I supposed to do, pull a Cher?"

"No, not saying that," she said and they laughed. "What I'm saying is," she said and paused. "Did you even call him?" she asked, following Kennedy into the back after she picked up her purse and keys. Kennedy put them down on her desk and Teresa was right on her heels.

"Nope."

"And why not?"

"Because you know, I don't want to seem desperate," she said, going back into the front of the store.

"But you are not desperate Kay," she said. They began to unlock the safes and filled the rest of the cases that Teresa had not filled yet.

"I don't know Ree, I'll call him, but I'll give it a little time."

"Okay whatever."

"What do you mean by that?"

"Listen Kay, you are my girl and I love you, but you've got to live a little. Take a chance on a man for once and stop looking at Cher and my crazy and unsuccessful relationships. Stop being afraid to get hurt," she said.

"I'm not afraid of being hurt," she said defensively.

"You are too," Teresa said as she closed the case she finished stocking. They were not quite set to open, but only had one or two more things to be taken out of the safe.

"I am not Ree. I just haven't found that right someone yet."

"How can you if you're not even dating? Men come in here all the time and I see men flirt with you or try to come on to you and you act like you are so busy or so uninterested."

"I am busy and most of the men that come up in here are buying gifts for their wives or girlfriends and then they got the nerve to ask for my number."

"Yeah, you're right about that," Teresa said and they laughed. "But, besides that, you haven't been on a date in what two, three years? I mean, I can't remember the last guy you went out with besides Travis and that wasn't what I'd consider to be a relationship," she said. Kennedy completely ignored her last statement about her and Travis.

"Look Ree, I hear you and I hear where you are coming from, but believe me, I'm not afraid of being hurt and I am not looking at the ins and outs of you and Cher's relationships. When the right fellow comes along I'll know it."

"Okay, well I hope you are paying attention," she said, looking at the man coming through the door.

Kennedy was down in the safe and she didn't see Julian coming into the unlocked door that she had forgotten to lock when she came in. The store was not open yet, but Julian saw Teresa and walked in.

"What do you mean?" she asked as she stood. She wanted to slap Teresa for not giving her a warning.

"Hey Kennedy how are you?" Julian asked.

"Julian…, what a surprise," she said, not expecting to see him.

"Yeah, I know right and you're Teresa right?" he asked, extended his hand and she smiled.

"Yes, hello," she said and they shook.

"I'm sorry to just drop by like this, but I didn't get your number. When you didn't call yesterday, I didn't want to take a chance on not talking to you again."

"Well I was going to call you, but you know…, yesterday…, I…, I…, was sorta busy," she said, fumbling over her words.

"Oh okay…, you know it's cool. I just didn't know what to think and you know you never can be too sure nowadays," he said.

Kennedy was speechless because he looked even more delicious in the day time than he looked the night she met him. She stood there not knowing what to say next. She saw Teresa ease away from the corner of her eye.

"Well listen Kennedy, I don't want to take up too much of your time and I can see you have to get back to work," he said, breaking the silence.

"No, no Julian you're not interrupting, you just caught me off guard. I didn't expect to see you this morning…, that's all."

"I know and again I didn't want to just drop in on you, but I thought about you yesterday and…," he began.

She couldn't believe her ears. *'I thought about you yesterday,'* was all she heard and she didn't hear anything else.

"Excuse me, I'm sorry," she said, snapping out of her trance.

"I was just wondering if you had dinner plans for tonight, maybe you and I can grab some dinner, if that's okay with you," he asked, repeating what he said because she didn't hear anything after, *'I thought about you yesterday.'*

"Dinner…, yeah…, dinner sounds good. I should be done here about six. Is that okay?"

"Six is perfect. Can I come back and pick you up, or would you rather meet me?"

"You can come back to get me. I mean, my truck will be fine here. If you want to do that, you can," she said nervously.

"Okay then I'll come by to pick you up," he said, backing away.

"Okay," she said, giving him a warm smile. "Oh, here is a card with my number. You know, in case anything changes," she said, grabbing one of her cards from the card holder on the counter.

He walked back toward her and she handed it to him. He glanced at it quickly and saw her cell number on it too and he smiled.

"You enjoy the rest of your day."

"You too," she said as he backed away and finally turned to walk out the door. She stood there frozen, unable to believe what had just happened. As soon as he was gone, Teresa came from the back.

"Girl, oooh my God…, see, I told you," Teresa said, squealing.

"Ree, what just happened?" Kennedy asked, still shocked

"Well my dear, a fine ass man just walked in and asked you to dinner."

"Yeah I know…, I got that part. I want to know, what made that miracle happen? No man has ever made me feel like that man just did a moment ago. I mean I must have looked retarded, not knowing what to say and stuttering like a fool."

"See…, what did I tell you?" Teresa asked, smiling.

"Hey, hey, okay. I hear you, but it's just dinner. Like I told you before he walked in not to get all geeked, I'm going to follow my own advice," she said, finally coming back to reality.

"Well my dear, all I can say is what's meant to happen gon' happen and there is nothing we can do about it."

"Well we have nothing to worry about then, do we?"

"I guess we don't," Teresa said and then they got to work.

For a Monday, the store was steady, but Kennedy kept looking at the clock and six o'clock seemed like it was never going to come. At 3:00, she started to get eager because Teresa was right, she hadn't been out to dinner or on a real date in ages. The only thing she hated was that she was dressed in her work attire, which was the normal black, blue, or navy skirt with a white, gray, or blue button down blouse. That day, she had on a black pencil skirt and a silk button down white blouse.

That was work appropriate, but definitely not dinner date appropriate, so she decided to hurry down the street to get something to change into, especially another pair of shoes because her work shoes were comfy, but not stylish.

"Hey Ree, can you handle things for me? I want to run down to the mall and get something else to wear."

"Oh okay, I see someone is starting to see this dinner for what it really is, a date."

"Hey look at me, look at my shoes. I don't want to go to dinner looking like I just came from church. I look like an usher," she said and they both laughed.

"Yeah you do. You may wanna hurry up."

"Okay, I'll be back as quickly as I can," she said, then grabbed her purse and jetted out of the door. She went right into Ashley Stewart because she knew it would be a waste of time going into any other store because plus size clothes were not the easiest to shop for.

She grabbed the first cute denim skirt and top that matched in her size and ran into the fitting room. The bottoms were perfect, but she had to go down a size on the top. She ran back to the rack and put the 18/20 back and snatched a 14/16 and at the counter she stood there smiling because she actually had a date.

She ran into the closest shoe store on that side of the mall. She didn't look long; she grabbed the first cute, size eight sandals that she saw. She was so glad that she had gotten her toes done that Friday evening, because otherwise sandals would have not been an option. She hurried back to the jewelry store and went into the bathroom and changed. She pulled out her make-up bag and put on a little make-up. She looked at her hair and knew that her little homemade French roll was going to have to do.

She took her comb out and pulled a few strands out on both sides of her head to add a little spice to her up-do. She realized she didn't have on any earrings or any other accessories and she thought to herself owning a jewelry store was the perfect thing for her at that moment. She went to the front and it was a quarter 'til six and Ree was getting ready to close out the register.

"Tiffany, can you start to put away the items in section F for me?" Ree asked.

Kennedy was so glad that she hired Teresa because she was not only a good friend, but she did a hell of a fine job for her. Everything that she wanted Teresa to take care of, she did and did it superbly.

"Hey Ree, I got to get a set to wear tonight."

"Are you getting it on loan or purchase?" she asked before she closed the register.

"You know, I think I will purchase that set over there in section K. I've been saying I'm going to get it since it came in, so I think I'm going to get it."

"Okay, bring me the sku and I'll get that in for you."

"Okay, just put it on the house account for me."

"Okay, no problem," she said and gave Kennedy a look.

"What?" Kennedy asked.

"Nothing, you look cute."

"Thanks Ree," she said and went over to the cabinet to get the earring and necklace set that she had been wanting for weeks. "Tiff, can you come and open this for me, my keys are in the back."

"Sure thing Ms. Banks," Tiffany said and opened the case for her.

"Can you give this to Teresa for me?" she said, taking the card from the bottom of the case with the sku number on it.

"Yes, no problem," she said as she locked the case. "So, Ms. Banks, you got a hot date?" Tiffany asked, in Kennedy's business.

She didn't socialize with any of her staff on that level, only Teresa, because they were friends in and outside of business. Kennedy didn't get offended nor did she say anything to Tiffany about her inquiring about her personal business, she just answered her.

"As a matter fact I do Tiffany. I have a dinner date."

"Well you look nice Ms. Banks. I have never seen you with make-up on."

"Tiffany, you've worked for me for three years, come on, I know you've seen me with make-up on before."

"No ma'am, lip gloss yes, but never made up like you are now," she said and Kennedy thought about it. She never made up her face for work, only press powder and lip gloss.

"Well I guess you haven't," she said and turned the mirror on the glass counter around and put on the earrings. She tried to put on the necklace, but was having a hard time.

"Let me get that for you," Tiffany offered and helped her.

"Thank you, Tiffany."

"No problem," she said and went over to Teresa and handed her the card so she could scan it.

"Thanks Tiffany, after you put away your sections you can go home," Teresa said to Tiffany.

"Okay, I'll be done in about ten minutes," she said, then went to finish her job.

Kennedy went back into the bathroom to check herself in the mirror once again and then she went into her office and waited for her clock to read six. She watched the camera's until he walked in. She got up and took a deep breath and headed for the door. She turned out the lights and said a silent prayer. Not that she was praying for her and Julian to get married or anything, she prayed that she didn't do anything to embarrass herself on their date.

She made her way to the front and when he saw her he stopped in the middle of his sentence and looked at her.

"Hello," he said.

"Hello Julian," she said back to him with a big smile and everyone stood still. Tiffany was over to the side trying to appear busy, but she was watching to see what was going down.

"Julian was telling me that he is not a jewelry man, he is only into watches," Teresa said.

"Yeah, that is what he told me too," Kennedy said, not being able to take her eyes off him.

"And I told him that we were going to have to change that," Teresa said, but it was like no one was paying her any attention.

"We will be working on that for sure," Kennedy said, still looking at Julian.

"You won't have to work hard Ms. Banks," he said and winked.

"Oh really?" she said, smiling.

"Yea, I don't think you have to do much to convince me," he replied.

"Well I see you two are ready to get better acquainted, so y'all should head out," Teresa advised.

"Yea, we should. Teresa I will see you tomorrow," Kennedy said and then moved to the other side of the counter.

"So, are you ready?" Julian asked.

"Yes, I'm ready," Kennedy said.

He took her hand. They headed out the door and Kennedy had to blink herself back to reality because that moment seemed unreal.

Chapter Five

"Thank you," Kennedy said to the server. She brought their drink order back quickly and remembered to bring the extra napkins that Kennedy asked her to bring.

"You're very welcome. Are you guys ready to order?" she asked nicely.

"No not yet. Give us a few moments please," Julian said to her. She nodded and proceeded to another table. "So, how was your day?" he asked.

"Long," Kennedy said, then took a sip of her merlot.

"Tell me about it. I was staring at the clock the entire afternoon," he said, being honest. He was anxiously waiting to meet Kennedy for dinner so he could see her sweet smile.

"Oh really?" she asked, looking at him like she thought he was joking.

"Yes, why would that surprise you?"

"Well I'm not surprised Julian, because I was watching the clock myself. I'm just kinda surprised that you actually admitted it," she said.

Not that she thought Julian was too fine to even think of her that way; she just wondered how she caught the attention of a man with such long, beautiful eye lashes. He had the longest eyelashes and the sexiest eyes she'd ever seen on a man. His low hair cut was not bald, but faded nicely and it looked both professional and sexy on him. He was maybe six feet or an inch shorter Kennedy figured. Kennedy preferred tall men because wearing a shoe or sandal without a heel was not an option since she was only 5'3."

Although he had on a loose fitting button down and loose

fitting blue jeans, Kennedy knew his body was right.

She watched his lips move and was impressed by his white and perfectly even teeth, but she didn't compliment him on it. She like men that were two shades darker, but his medium brown skin had a hint of red, so she figured he may have a native back grown.

He wore a nicely trimmed mustache with a nicely shaped beard and she liked that because it laid so nicely and complimented his masculine jaw line. He put you in mind of a Columbus Short, the guy from *Stomp the Yard*, but he was definitely taller and a little more distinguished looking.

"Oh okay, so you don't look for honesty?" he asked, then sipped his Crown on the rocks, bringing her back to the conversation from her brief moment of admiring thoughts.

"Yes, but do I usually get it that? No," she said, making him laugh again.

"Well I'm not gon' front or lie. I do my best to tell the truth, except when it is necessary to lie," he said and Kennedy gave him a curious look.

"When is it necessary to lie Julian?" she asked, interested in what his answer would be.

"Well if your life is on the line, you gon' have to lie to save your ass, or if you need something that you just have to have and you have no other way of getting it, you may have to lie. In my opinion, a lie can get you in and out of a world of trouble."

"So, you will lie to keep yourself out of trouble?"

"Yea, I would," he said and they both laughed a little.

"I guess you are right. No one would actually stand there and tell the truth if they knew that they are going to be in a world of trouble."

"Exactly," he said and the waitress came over again.

"Have you guys decided yet?" she asked, ready to take their order.

"Actually, we haven't looked over our menus yet. Can we please have a few more moments?" he asked.

"Sure, not a problem. Just wave when you guys are ready," she said with a pleasant smile and quickly walked over to her other table.

"So, would you lie to your woman to save your ass?" she

asked curiously.

"Well if she is my woman and we are serious, I wouldn't lie to her. If she asked me a question like 'do I look fat in this?' or if it is something that will hurt her feelings, of course I'm gon' lie through my teeth," he said.

"Well if I'm ever your woman I want to know the truth, even if it hurts."

"Really?" he asked, wondering if she really meant that.

"Yes, I don't want to be sugar coated or babied. I am a woman and I have to take the good with the bad."

"Oh, so you are tough huh, Ms. Kennedy?"

"Well my momma died when I was fifteen and I was raised by my daddy and my two uncles. I have three male cousins and Cherae was my only female influence growing up and trust, she and I are total opposite."

"Okay, I see you are a force to be reckoned with?"

"No I wouldn't say that, but after my momma died, my daddy wasn't like a pillow. He spoiled me yes and gave me anything and everything I wanted, but I had to work for it. I got good grades and did what I was supposed to do by him, so he had me rotten, but at the same time my daddy always warned me about boys and men. He made sure that I knew that men come and go and some men have no mercy on your heart," she said and took another sip of her drink.

"Damn, yo' daddy didn't sugar coat a thing, did he?"

"Nope and I'm glad he didn't."

"So, when was your last relationship?"

"Well let's just say I've never had a relationship to last longer than three or four months."

"Really?" he asked.

"Afraid so," she said, looking over her menu. She was afraid of the next question.

"Why?" he asked. She knew that was coming.

"I have a very low tolerance for men who want more than one woman."

"Oh, I see," he said and sipped his drink. He opened his menu and tried to decide on something to eat. "Well I believe that people should be up front and say what it is they are looking for so there are no misunderstandings in the long run."

"True, however, when you met a person and they tell you that they are looking for something long term and you're not, I think that you shouldn't get involved."

"Not necessarily Kennedy," he said, closing his menu.

"Well Julian, if you are looking to just have a fling? Why involve yourself with someone who is looking for more?"

"Well for one, just because you may not be looking for something serious at the moment, the person you may be kicking it with may be the person you start to want to be with. You can be looking for something long term just like the next person and you could end up with a person that wasn't worth your time, so you should go into it looking to be happy and whatever transpires is what you deal with."

"That's true too Julian, but in my opinion, a man or woman that is still interested in dating other people and keeping their options open usually end up hurting the person that is ready to have a committed relationship."

"Yea, I guess that is true too," he said. "Have you figured out what you want to have?"

"Yeah, I think I'm ready," she said and he waived for the waitress. They ordered their meals and continued nonstop conversation while they waited. He definitely liked Kennedy and her conversation and although he thought she was tough and a bit uptight, something about her made him want to get to know her.

He would have never thought of Kennedy as someone he'd date, but the connection was there from their first conversation and he couldn't deny that found her interesting. At the same time, she was still trying to figure him out and see if she'd detect a hint of bullshit from him or if he was genuine. He seemed nice and seemed to be a descent guy, but she knew they all started out that way.

"So, how did you get started in the nightclub business?" she asked as the waitress refilled their water.

"Well I own a couple restaurants and a friend of mine who is a realtor keep me posted on opportunities and the previous club owner didn't make good on it and the bank sold it for a good price."

"Oh okay, so do like owning the club?"

"Yeah, I'm getting use to it. It's a lot different from my restaurants and a lot of staying up late," he said.

"Yea, I bet."

"But for the most part, it's cool."

"Well I wish your spot had something going on during the week.

"Like?" he asked, wondering what she had in mind.

"I don't know. Jazz night, ole school Sundays, just something other than the club on Friday and Saturday night."

"Yea, but will people come?"

"Well if you start letting people know in advance, you know, maybe you can get some feedback to see what the people want. You know, try it a couple months and see how it goes."

"Well that sounds good. I hadn't thought about it, but that is a good idea," he said and she smiled. "So, Miss Kennedy, how old are you?" he asked.

She hesitated for a moment. "Now you know it's inappropriate to ask a woman her age," she said and sipped her drink.

"You know, I've always wondered why women find that so offensive," he said.

She decided to tell him why. "Well Mr. Roberson, women like to look as young as they can and when you ask a woman how old she is when you know she is definitely over the age of eighteen, we feel that maybe men think that we are old or look older than what we really are," she tried to explain, but didn't think she explained it well enough.

"Oh I see, but let me tell you this Ms. Banks. We are not thinking that way at all. It's just a matter of knowing how old you really are. I think you look like you are in your late twenties or early thirties, but I can't pin point your age to the exact number, therefore, I have to ask," he said.

She didn't feel that offensiveness she had been taught as a woman after he explained it to her.

"Well Julian, I'm thirty four, was born February nineteenth," she said smiling.

"Really, my birthday is February eighteenth," he said. He

found that interesting.

"So, you are an Aquarius? Couldn't wait one more day to be a Pisces huh," she said.

"Nope, my momma said I was so anxious to get here, she was only in labor for two hours," he joked and she was enjoying him.

The server brought out their meals. "Is there anything else I can get for you guys?" she asked with a smile.

"No, we are good, unless you need something?" Julian asked Kennedy.

"Another glass of wine would be great," she said and Julian ordered another drink too. "So, your parents are they still together?" she asked.

"Nope, my dad left when I was six. I have one sister she lives out in Tinley Park," he said. She nodded because her mouth was full. "So, how did your mom die?

"Cancer," she said and took a sip of her wine. "It was difficult, but my dad was awesome, you know. He is just like my best friend now since my momma passed and I can talk to him about everything. We are close," she said, not wanting to bring the mood down with conversation about her dead mother.

"Yea, I hear ya. You growing up without your mom made you and your dad close and me growing up without my dad definitely made me and my mom close. I have a couple of nephews and my sister and I are tight, but I do wish I had my dad around," he said, being honest.

"Just like I wish my mom was still here too," she said. They were silent for a while and finished their meals.

When the waitress cleared the table the mood went back to the mood they had before discussing her mom and his dad. They continued to talk and realized how late it was getting and they decided to head back to Kennedy's truck.

Chapter Six

It was Saturday and Kennedy was in a very good mood. She was walking around with a smile the entire day. She and Julian had gone out each night the week before and she had plans to go to the club that night. She left the store early that afternoon and planned to go home and rest, but she was so energetic she cleaned the house and went to the car wash to clean her Denali. When she finally sat down it was only eight and she had a few hours before heading to the club. She asked Cherae if she wanted to go, but she said she was staying in and Kennedy didn't argue because Teresa had already agreed to go with her.

When she was in the bathroom putting on her make-up, Cherae came in dressed and ready to go. "I thought you said you were staying in?" Kennedy asked.

"I was, but I decided not to. Hell, why should a diva like myself stay in the house on a Saturday night? Shit, it ain't like I gotta date," Cherae said. She shut the lid, sat on the toilet and watched Kennedy apply her make-up.

"I know that's right," Kennedy said, co-signing what her girlfriend said. Although she felt Cherae was nowhere near diva status, she went along with her.

"So, is your boyfriend gon' let us in free because I'm a little short on cash?" Cherae said.

"Well Cher, I didn't ask him that, but if you are short, I gotcha," Kennedy said and walked out of the bathroom. She was not happy with Cher always needing money, but she wasn't stingy so she didn't give Cherae a hard time. She stepped into her jeans and went into her walk in closet and grabbed three pairs of sandals.

"Cher, which one should I wear?" she asked, trying on one pair at a time.

"The tan ones," Cherae answered.

"Are you sure, because my shirt is not quite this tan?" she said, second guessing her.

"Yea, I'm sure. These don't match," she said, picking up one of the other sandals. "And the brown ones are ugly," she said with a frown on her face.

"The brown ones are not ugly Cher," Kennedy said, examining them on her feet. The brown ones were the cute pair in her opinion.

"Whatever, I say the tan."

"Okay, I'll wear the tan ones," she said and finished dressing.

She and Cherae headed to the club and when they got there, Teresa was in the parking lot waiting for them. When they got up to the door, Julian appeared out of nowhere.

"Hey ladies, come on in," he said, moving the velvet rope aside so they could pass through.

"Thank you Julian," Kennedy said.

"Not a problem and I have a table for you and your friends," he said.

They followed and Cher was eyeing him up and down before she spoke. "Hey handsome, how ya been?" Cher asked him as if Kennedy wasn't there.

"I've been good...., Cherae, right?" he asked as if he was making sure that was her name.

"Yes, but please call me Cher," she said seductively. Kennedy wanted to yank her ass.

"Ok then Cher," he said. He turned his attention back to Kennedy. "And how are you? So glad you made it."

"Well I couldn't pass up the opportunity to see you again," she said and smiled.

"Okay...," he said smiling back, but remembered the bad news. "Well babe, I am not going to be able to spend too much time with you tonight because I'm short staffed, so I'm going to be all over the place."

"Oh it's okay," she said a little disappointed, but she

41

smiled.

"I'll send one of the waitresses over and you ladies order whatever you want," he said to all of them.

"Oh, what I want ain't on the menu," Cherae said, flirting again.

"Thank you Julian," Kennedy intermittent, giving Cher the evil eye.

"Okay, I'll be around if you need me," he told Kennedy as he walked off.

"Cher what the hell was that?" Kennedy asked angrily.

"What? What are you talking about?"

"Cher, come on, you were flirting with him right in front of Kay's face," Teresa said.

"Thank you," Kennedy said.

"Chile please, ain't nobody flirting with him and besides, he ain't her man."

"Not yet..., and I won the draw, so chill out Cher," Kennedy spat. "You know the rules and it's not cool for you to be batting yo' eyes and hitting on him.

"Hold on Kay, don't even. I am not flirting with him. I'm just being me, so if you think it's that serious. Step up yo' game."

"You know what Cher, I love you like a sister and if you have any respect for our friendship you will chill the fuck out and honor the draw. Meaning I don't have to step up my game."

"Okay, okay. Damn Kay, I was just having a little fun. Don't be mad at me. I love you and I'd never disrespect the draw," she said and then reached over to hug Kennedy.

"Okay Cher, I like this guy, so please...," Kennedy expressed.

"Okay Kay, I hear you boo."

"Alright," Teresa said.

The waitress came over and they put in their drink orders. The club was jumping and they were ready to have a good time. Kennedy enjoyed herself, but was highly disappointed that Julian was too busy to even dance one song with her. She had very brief conversations with him because he was on the move. When the DJ called last call, she was sitting at the table by herself, wondering if he'd at least dance with her one song before the night ended.

Cher was nowhere to be found and Teresa's friend she met the week prior was there. They were sitting in the corner talking in each other's ear. Kennedy sat there alone, wondering if she should have never gone because her main reason for going out that night was to see Julian. After about ten minutes of her sitting there alone, the DJ decided to slow it down. He played Chris Brown *'Poppin'*, after that, he played Ne-Yo and Jennifer Hudson *'Leaving Tonight.'* That was Kennedy's song, but she sat there 'til it ended without anyone asking her to dance. After he played that, he went back to the old school and played the O'Jays *'Hooks in Me.'* She was sitting there, waiting for at least one person to ask her to dance.

When the song was coming to an end, she figured she'd call it a night and find her girls so she could roll, but he finally came to her table. The DJ played Lauryn Hill and De'Angelo, *'Nothing Even Matters,'* and he asked her to dance. She smile and took his hand and he held her close as they danced slowly to the smooth groove that had her feeling high. He squeezed her body as she stayed close to him and didn't want the song to end, but all good things do come to an end, she thought, when the lights came on.

"I'm sorry I didn't get to spend time with you tonight," he said when he walked her back to the table.

"It's okay, I understand. Business is business and duty calls," she said and gave him a warm smile.

"Listen Kennedy, I am going to be here for a while because I have to help close up, but I really want to see you tonight when I get off," he said. It sent chills up and down her spin.

"Well Julian, how late are we talking?" she asked.

"Honestly, I don't know. I will try to wrap up as soon as possible. Can I call you?" he asked. She didn't speak; she just nodded her head up and down. "Okay, I will call you as soon as I'm done. We can meet me for breakfast. It is all up to you."

"Okay, just call me. I have to take Cher home, so call me."

"I will," he said and gave her a quick peck on the lips. She was so mesmerized by him, she stood there frozen for a moment or two after he walked away.

Chapter Seven

The next morning, Kennedy was completely dressed. She was in her bed on top of the covers and it took her a moment, but she finally realized she went to sleep waiting to hear from Julian. She grabbed her phone and she had five missed calls. She wanted to kick herself because they were all from Julian and she had missed him. '*How in the hell did I not hear my phone?*' she asked herself and then she realized it was on vibrate. "Damn, damn, damn," she said out loud and got up to go to the bathroom.

When she went to the sink to wash her hands, her reflection almost made her jump. One side of her hair was looking like Scary Spice and her smeared lipstick look like she had done her make up in the dark. She grabbed a fresh wash cloth from her linen closet and washed her face. She didn't bother brushing her hair, she just started the shower. She peeled off her clothes and stepped in. Feeling so disappointed for missing Julian's calls, she stood there and let the hot water just run over her head and body.

After shampooing her hair and lathering up one more good time, she got out. She put on her robe, went into her room and turned on some music. She went back into the bathroom and combed through her wet hair and contemplated if she should blow it dry or sit under the hot ass dryer for a while. Not feeling like doing either, she just combed it back and headed downstairs for something to eat.

When she went into the kitchen, Cher was in there cooking in some teeny, weenie boxer briefs and a cut off tee shirt.

"Good morning, superstar," she said to Cher.

"Good morning. I didn't know you were here."

"Well I missed his called. My stupid phone was on vibrate," Kennedy said and poured herself a glass of orange juice.

"Aw, man, I thought you were gonna have a juicy story to tell this morning."

"What?"

"You know, I just thought for sure you were gon' give that brotha some last night. The way you were carrying on, on the ride home."

"I was not carrying on," Kennedy said, defending herself.

"Chile please, yes you were. Julian is so sweet and girl, Julian said this and the other day he said that...yuck," Cher said, sounding jealous.

"Well he is sweet Cher and just because I said all those things doesn't mean I was going to give him some."

"Yea, that's what yo' mouth says," she said, pulling a plate from the cabinet.

"Whatever," Kennedy said; lifting her head to see what Cher was cooking. "What are you making and is there enough for me?"

"Girl, I made me an omelet with everything and I'm sorry, this is only enough for me and I'm not sharing."

"Come on Cher, we can half it."

"Nope, you might wanna fix your own."

"See I wouldn't do you like that."

"I normally wouldn't do you like this either, but I'm hungry and if I'da known you were here, I'da made you one" she said and sat down to eat her huge omelet by herself."

"Fine, then I'll make myself something," she said, getting up and going to the fridge. She grabbed a few things and rinsed the skillet that Cher used to make herself an omelet, because Cher's sure looked good. "I can't understand how you can eat everything under the sun and still not gain a pound," Kennedy said to Cher while she cracked her eggs.

"Girl it's genetic, or maybe I'm just blessed," Cher said, boasting.

"Yea, I guess."

"Well maybe if you worked out a little."

"For what? I'm not complaining. I'm thick and fine, baby.

Skinny doesn't make you pretty."

"Hump, okay," Cher said, eating her omelet like she wanted to finish it before someone took it away from her.

"So, what are you saying Cher?" Kennedy asked. She knew Cherae thought of herself as the cream of the crop, but never did she think she thought for a second that she was unattractive.

"Nothing Kay, nothing," she said, avoiding that subject.

"You meant something Cher," Kennedy said, looking her square in the eye.

"Nothing, I mean, you are pretty and all Kay, but back in the day when you were smaller, you were more appealing…, that's all," she said, not making eye contact with her.

"Says who?" Kennedy asked with attitude.

"Says nobody Kay, it's just my opinion."

"Whatever Cher, everybody's not meant to be the same size and none like you, not all of us are perfect," Kennedy said.

Not that she cared about Cher's opinion, but her feelings were kind of hurt. Kennedy didn't have hang ups about her weight because she felt just as beautiful as Cher, but hearing something like that from her best friend made her feel like she wasn't pretty.

"Kay damn, don't be getting all emotional and don't be taking it like that. You know I think you are pretty, but in my opinion, a few years back before you gained a few pounds here and there, I think you were more attractive," she told her being honest. Kennedy didn't flinch because she preferred a person's honesty over a lie.

"Well my dear, whether I've gained a few pounds here and there, I still know that I'm beautiful inside and out and I don't have to have a man to certify that every five minutes. So, if you think I was more attractive when I was a size twelve verses a sixteen that is your opinion. My daddy raised me to know who I am so if I'm a twelve, a sixteen, twenty, or twenty eight, Kennedy will still be beautiful because even if my clothes sizes change, I'm still going to be Kennedy Renee Fine Ass Banks," she said with pride.

All she could think to herself was the nerve of her. Just because she was a four on a good day didn't make her more beautiful than Kennedy. And, let the truth be told, all Cherae had going for herself was her beauty because she was broke with no

46

ambition, no direction and didn't have a passion for anything in life other than a mirror. The only thing she loved more than herself was money; correction, other people's money because money didn't motivate her to make her own.

"Look Kay, I'm sorry. I didn't mean to say anything to hurt your feelings okay? We've been friends forever and you've always told me, *'Cher, always be honest, tell me the truth, even if it hurts,'*" she told Kennedy.

"It's okay Cher," Kennedy said, chopping her vegetables for her omelet. "I'm not mad nor am I offended and as always, I appreciate you being honest. What kind of a friend would you be if you couldn't tell me the truth?" she said.

Cher didn't say anything. She just finished her food and Kennedy cooked in silence. They ate in silence and when they were done with their food, Kennedy went back up to her room and Cherae went to hers.

When Kennedy was done blow drying her hair, she decided to give Julian a call. When he didn't answer she was disappointed, but she went on and left a message. She looked at the clock and it was still a little before eleven, so she figured he may have still been sleeping. She put on some shorts and an oversized shirt and decided to do a couple loads of clothes. She grabbed her hamper from the bathroom and removed the lid to begin sorting her clothes and she saw her cell phone spinning on her nightstand. She thought to herself, *'Damn, I still didn't take my phone off vibrate'*.

She made a mad dash to get her phone and realized it was Julian calling her back. She sat on the bed and took a deep breath before she answered.

"Hello," she said smiling.

"Good morning, how are you?"

"I'm good and how about you?"

"Well let's just say disappointed."

"I know, but let me tell you what happened," she said smiling, glad to hear from him.

"Oh boy here we go," he said, teasing.

"What do you mean, Julian? I told you I live by the rule of honesty."

"Okay then Miss Honest, what happened?"

"I fell asleep," she said and he burst into laughter. "Julian, I did. I came in and I laid across my bed waiting for you and I fell asleep."

"And where was your phone? I called you five times, my dear," he said, dying to hear her response.

"It was on vibrate and I didn't know. I forgot to turn the volume up."

"Okay and that's the truth?"

"Yes that's the truth," she said nervously. It was the truth, but she felt like he wasn't going to believe her.

"Okay, I'm just messing with you. I believe you," he said and she relaxed. "So, what are you up to today?"

"Nothing much, was about to do a little laundry, nothing big," she said, looking over at her hamper.

"So, how about you let me take you somewhere today?"

"You can take me somewhere," she said smiling.

"Well how about I pick you up at 1:00 and we spend some time together today. I wanna take you to a couple of my restaurants to sample some of my specialties."

"Okay, I'd like that. I didn't know you had specialties, so my answer is yes," she said, going straight to her closet to see what she was going to wear.

"Okay then, I'll see you soon," he said.

They hung up and the first thing she did was take her phone off vibrate. She went for her cute jeans and a little cute strapless top. She stood in the mirror and flat ironed her hair in her half bra and jeans and she thought about what Cher said to her that morning about not being attractive at her size. She turned to the side, examined herself, shook it off and said, "I look good," with a smile on her face. She applied her make-up thinking out loud. *"Nobody's perfect and I'm sexy just the way I am,"* she said and admired her beautiful hair, made up face and round hips in her jeans. She grabbed her top to put it on and she heard the doorbell.

Chapter Eight

Cherae woke up early that morning. She was nervous and biting her nails because she hadn't paid the light bill for two months and she was scared that the power company was going to pull the plug. She went the entire week hoping that God would allow her more time before Com-Ed made a trip out to their house. She was walking around the house on edge, wondering how she was going to come up with the money that Kennedy had given her last month and the month before. That money was in her closet hanging on her shoe rack. She had bought shoes instead, both times and had it in her mind that one of her guys would save her again.

Crazy thing was, she had gotten the money back four times from her male sponsors, but unable to resist spending the money on herself, she still neglected to pay the electric bill. With not enough money and no one else to ask, she was so nervous she thought she would pass out. She went into the kitchen and looked out the window and noticed Kennedy's Denali was gone. She wondered where she was that early on a Saturday morning. She walked around the house nervously, but smiled at herself every time she passed a mirror. She would admire herself and thought she had to find a rich husband quickly before she started to sag. She wanted to always be able to walk around in sexy pajamas, showing off her everything.

She knew she wouldn't be able to get away with telling people she was thirty for long. She was coming up on thirty-four soon and she had to get her a husband quick. She didn't understand how she could not have found the right one yet. Either they were sweet and paid more than enough attention to her but didn't have enough money or they had the money, but they treated her like she was property. Men with money were very controlling because they knew they had power. All she would be was their trophy, the woman that they loved having on their arm to show off.

She was growing tired of how her life was going. She wished she had listened to Kennedy and went to school. She wished she hadn't wasted her time trying to get by on her looks, which worked for her for a long time, but now she was not as hot as she used to be and it was like she wasn't coming across the generous type of brothers anymore. She was wearing out her welcome with some of her old, call on me anytime sponsors and she was starting to feel disgusted with being with the oldie but goodies that lavished her with anything because they smelled funny and they were just plain old.

She paced the floor and thought really hard on which one of her male supporters she could call to get $380.00 dollars from to bring their electric bill current, but couldn't come up with anyone. She thought about asking Cortez, but she knew it was too soon to be asking him to break her off that amount of money. She tossed the idea around in her head of asking him anyway and since she was so desperate, she had to ask him. She figured all he could do was say no. Hell, she had been fucking him since the night they met. He owed her at least $300.00 of it, she thought to herself.

She went into her room and hunted for her cell phone. She walked back toward the kitchen to make the call because she wanted to watch out for Kennedy. She didn't want her to walk in on her conversation. She dialed his number and when he picked up, she suddenly felt nervous and was having second thoughts. That wasn't like her because she was quick to have her hand out.

"Hey, Cortez, this is Cherae. How are you?" she asked, trying to sound cool.

"Hey Cherae, I'm good, how are you?"

"I'm okay, I've seen better days."

"Yeah we all have," he joked and she laughed a little.

"Hey, I was just calling because I had a huge favor to ask you," she said before she lost her nerve.

"What's up? What do you need?"

"Well under normal circumstances I wouldn't ask, but last night my girls and I went out and you not gon' believe me when I tell you this, but I lost my purse or someone stole it. I'm not sure," she said, lying through her teeth.

"That is horrible."

"I know, tell me about. That leads me to my next question. I had about $500.00 dollars with me and I know it was so stupid of me to have that kinda loot on me, but it was for a couple of bills and I can't dare ask my girl for that kinda money and who knows the mess I'm gonna have to clear up with my account and credit cards. I got to take care of some things and I was wondering," she tried to say, but he didn't allow her to finish.

"Sure, not a problem, I just hope you can get your other stuff cleared and not lose a lot more than that behind this. Man that is terrible."

"I know and worst part is how you can just swipe your card now where ever and you know a lot of these places don't really check any I.D. All of my identification is in my wallet and I know some heifer out there trying to impersonate me."

"Yeah you are right, but at least I know you canceled your credit cards and called your bank?" he asked, truly concerned.

"With the quickness," she said, lying. All of her cards were to the limit. If her purse was actually stolen, the theft would be embarrassed if he tried to purchase anything on her.

"Yeah, well don't worry. If your bank is anything like my bank, they got you covered."

"Yea, I hope so," she said, feeling one hundred pounds lighter. She had the money to pay the electric and a couple dollars for her pocket, so she was feeling pretty good.

They talked a little while longer and he agreed to come by later to bring her the money. She got off the phone jumping up and down. She went over to the mirror to have a conversation with herself, *"You still got it, girlfriend, so shake that money maker,"* she said, dancing to her own conceited beat that played in her head. She turned to the side, watched her ass giggle and she thought she was the epitome of beauty. She was about to continue her routine, but the door bell ranged.

She didn't think twice about how underdressed she was and

sashayed to the door. She went up on her tip toes and peeped out the peephole and said to herself, '*today truly is my lucky day*,' when she saw that it was Julian. She unlocked the door, trying not to seem too excited, but she was so glad she had an opportunity to have him alone without Kennedy and even though her attempts were subtle before, she could say how she really felt with Kennedy not being in ears distance.

"Hey Julian, how are you?" she said, smiling seductively.

"I'm fine," he said, returning a smile. Although his smile was innocent, the evil one she carried was the complete opposite.

"You can say that again," Cherae said, not playing the role.

"Is Kennedy home? I didn't see her truck. I was supposed to meet her here."

"No, she's not here, but you are welcome to come in and wait for her. I can keep you company while you wait." she said, opening the door wider so he could get a better view of her half dressed body.

He knew already what he was dealing with and he wasn't about to go out like that. Cher had been flirting and coming at him since the night he met them and although he showed interest in her best friend, that didn't stop Cher at all and she truly irritated him.

"No, I'll just come back in a few," he said, turning to walk away. Cherae was just about to flex and lure him in, but she saw Kennedy's Denali from the corner of her eye and decided to step back.

"Okay, suit yo' self," she said and hurried to shut the door. She made a mad dash to her room to put on some sweats; she definitely didn't want to hear a word out of Kennedy's mouth about putting on something more appropriate.

Chapter Nine

Kennedy was feeling good. She and Julian were hanging more and more and she loved it. It had been a little over three months since they had started going out and she knew it was time to lay out the red carpet for him. They kissed and played around a little on Kennedy's sofa a few times, but he had never gone up to her room. She had been by his place, but never stayed the night, so she was ready to initiate some physical contact between them.

She stopped by the mall after work and went into Bath and Body Works to pick out some new fragrances. She was walking around smiling and wondering what it would be like to be with Julian. She hadn't done it in a long, long time and she was ready to be with him. She smiled and thought back to the days when she used to mess around with Travis and realized she hadn't forgotten how to perform. She and Travis used to get down, but Travis was not feeling her in any way other than the bedroom. They went out, but rarely, so she couldn't lie and say that he was her man. He would schedule visits to see her or for her to come see him, but it would always be in the night hours.

It took Kennedy a long time to let that one go because his dick was top of the line dick. The kind you need a twelve step program to get off of, but she grew tired of fronting with her friends like their relationship was more than what it was. She didn't like lying so she never made up stories about their status, but she never denied when they said Travis was her boyfriend. The way he used to put it down she wished he was her man, but she was not naïve or slow. She knew he may have actually had a woman, but he and she made music in the bedroom together. That was all they had in common, except for eating late. That was when she put on a few pounds here and there. She kicked it with Travis for about two and a half years and all he did was fuck her and feed her. She'd stop in the middle of the night on her way home from his apartment and get fast food. He'd bring food with him when he came over and they would eat and head up to do what they knew he came to do.

Even when she noticed her clothes were getting snugger, she still did what made her feel good with Travis and that was, fuck and eat. After all the good sex and good eating, she wanted more. She started to grow tired of what they had going on and finally told Travis that they could no longer kick it. Getting off her addiction to his dick was substituted with more eating and unfortunately, but not painfully, by the time she got over him, she was already a sixteen. She wasn't mad at herself because she still turned a few heads and men still hit on her at the jewelry store from time to time.

She'd have very brief, '*I'm going on a diet,*' kicks. It would last for two good weeks and then she'd be back to normal. Cher always bugged her to go and workout with her and would always ask Kennedy, *"Why do you buy so much junk?"* Kennedy would look at her and say, *"You ask me that a million times, but I don't see you holding back on eating the junk."* Cherae would stuff her mouth with whatever treat she had and respond, *"But, I can do that though."* Kennedy felt that that was her nice way of saying, *"I'm not the one with the weight problem."*

So to avoid Cherae's dreams of her becoming a skinny girl conversation she'd just quickly change the subject, by complimenting Cherae on something. That was an easy diversion because Cherae loved talking about herself. Hell, Kennedy was surprised she had made it that long without being a full fledge big girl because her momma was a heavy woman, but as her daddy would say, *"She was the finest woman on the planet."*

She remembered overhearing her daddy and two uncles talking about women. She was serving them some chips and dip and getting them a cold beer to replace the empty cans on the table while they played cards. They all like women that were meaty and had some '*cushion for the pushing,*' she recalled her uncle Kendell saying. While they laughed and carried on about the love of a good woman, her daddy made a remark that had her uncles and even her, laughing for hours. They were telling her daddy how he should get back out there and date because her momma had passed about three years prior and she would never forget her daddy saying to his older brother, Keith, *"Man, don't be trying to hook me up with nobody, especially not no skinny chick and if you bring any woman around here for me she betta have some meat on her bones, because if she thick, she dead. I'd beat it death, boy I swear."* Kennedy almost dropped the bowl of pretzels on the floor.

She and her uncle's were laughing so hard. Although she missed her momma, she didn't like seeing her daddy alone and she was old enough to know that having someone to love and share your life with was important. She was old enough to know that her daddy was lonely and maybe needed some love or just some good loving in his life.

Although she knew her daddy had to have a gal out there somewhere, he had never introduced her to another woman and he had never mentioned one. Even when she would ask her daddy would say, *"Yo momma was the only woman for me."* She knew that was true, but her daddy was fine and had money, so she knew that somebody out there was pleasing him.

Hell, truth be told, if Cher could have pushed up on her daddy, she was sure she would have. She would see how Cher would be around her daddy. Even though her daddy treated Cher like she was his daughter too. If Cher could have had her way, she'd definitely be calling him daddy. Cher would never out right say it, but she would always say, *"Damn, Kay, Mr. Kenneth is fine. If he wasn't yo' daddy, he would definitely be my sugar daddy."* Kennedy would just look at her and shake her head. She was glad to know that Cher had some of the sense that God had given her not to even go there.

Kennedy left the mall and headed home. When she got in her truck, she called Julian to confirm their date for that night. He asked her could she come by the club to meet him and she agreed. She went home and took a nice, long bath and made sure she lotion up with her new Bath and Body Works. She topped it off with her body spray and rechecked the mirror ten times before she was finally ready to go. When she got downstairs, Cher was dressed too.

"Oh, so you're going out?" Kennedy asked.

"Yeah, Cortez is on his way," she said, frowning.

"Cortez huh? I think you like this one," Kennedy said, teasing.

"No he is the only one who asked me tonight."

"Well I see he likes you then," she said, trying to make her way to the door.

"Yeah whatever, I take it you are going out with Julian?"

"Yep, I sure am," Kennedy said, checking her make-up in the foyer mirror. The light was so much brighter than in her bathroom.

"So, I guess you plan on finally giving him some? What has it been three, four months?" Cher asked, being funny.

"Three Cher and maybe tonight is the night. What's it to you?" Kennedy asked, taking out her keys. Cher acted funny when it came to Julian and Kennedy didn't get her.

"Watch him Kay. I don't trust him. I know his type."

"Cher you've never been around Julian for more than a couple hours at a time, so how are you going to say that about him?"

"Okay, but don't say I didn't warn you," she said, throwing up her hands.

"I won't," Kennedy said and opened the door. "Have fun and tell Cortez I said hello," she said and closed the door behind her.

Chapter Ten

"Is this mic on?" Kennedy asked Johnson and tapped it.

"Yea, it's on. What you gon' do, spit some hot lyrics?" he asked, looking through his records as if he was looking for a particular album.

"Maybe," Kennedy said, holding the mic and looking around to see what ears were in listening distance. She was a bit shy and she didn't do well in front of a lot of people.

"Ok," Johnson said looking through his albums. "What's your flava? Some Jill Scott, Angie Stone, Tamia, or are you ole school?" he asked.

"How about Lauren Hill, do you have something from her?" she asked, thinking of what songs she actually knew all the words to.

"Cool, let me see what I got for ya," he said, pulling out an instrumental record of Lauren Hill's, *Ex-Factor*. It was an old cut, but Kennedy knew the lyrics to it. "Let's see what you got," he said and removed the vinyl from its cover. He put the record on the turn table and gently placed the needle on it. The music began to play and Kennedy smiled and waited until it was time to recite the first verse.

"It could all be so simple, but you'd rather make it hard. Loving you is like a battle and we both end up with scars." She sang and Johnson was shocked to hear the sounds that came out of her mouth. He didn't know she was walking around with a set of cords. He'd always see her with Julian, but had no idea she was vocally inclined.

"Care for me, care for me, said you'd be there for me, live

for me," she sang.

Julian realized that it was not Lauren's voice and he emerged from the back storage. He looked and was taken by surprise when he saw the mic in Kennedy's hand. He saw her up in the DJ booth singing into the mic better than the one and only Lauren Hill herself. He had no idea Kennedy could sing. That was a conversation that they never had.

He stood there and waited 'til she finished and applauded when the music ended. When Kennedy noticed that he had heard her she instantly had an embarrassing feeling come all over her body. She had a beautiful voice, but was one of those people who didn't walk around broadcasting her talents to everyone she came in contact with. She was modest and secretive about the gift she was blessed with.

She was so bored waiting for Julian to finish up at the club she just messed around with Johnson because besides him and Tony, she didn't know anyone else there that she could talk to. Singing was her momma's thang and she sat in smoked filled rooms for years singing with her band. Cancer crept up on her after years of entertaining with her voice and that was why Kennedy wasn't crazy in love with her talent.

"Damn, Kennedy, I didn't know you could blow like that," Johnson said as she put the mic back on its stand.

"Well I don't go around singing for everyone," Kennedy said shyly.

"Shit, you should. Your ass can sing girl," he said and Julian came up behind her.

"Kennedy, damn, baby, you didn't tell me that you could sing."

"Because I don't sing, Julian, I was just messing around."

"That didn't sound like you were messing around, that sounded like you were trying to put down a track on a CD," he teased.

Kennedy felt shy all over again. "Come on Julian that was okay. I know I do alright," she said modestly.

"No baby, you were '*sangin*'," he said and they laughed.

"Stop it Julian," she said humbly again.

"No baby seriously, you got a voice on you. Why haven't

you sang for me before?" he asked.

"Well I was hoping to sing for you tonight," she said seductively.

Johnson titled his head with a look of confusion. He had some idea of what was going on, but it was not what he really wanted to see, so he took the head phones off and quickly made his exit.

"Oh you were?" Julian asked and moved closer to her.

He was attracted to Kennedy and wanted her, but she was different from what he was used to. She was heavier than any woman he had ever dated and it was a relief for him, because she wasn't the high maintenance, divalicious type he had normally gone out with. Women like Cherae were the type of women he normally hooked up with and dated, but caused him the most problems. That was one of the reasons why when he met them, Cherae was the last thing on his mind.

When Kennedy came over to his table, he wasn't thinking of her as someone he would ask out or even attempt to date, but she was so smart and had great conversation that he wanted to continue to be in her presence. Being physically attractive to her was not progressing as fast as his mental attraction to her that was one of the reasons why he was moving as slow as he was. He did like her, but she was definitely not the type of woman he normally hooked up with.

He went back and forth in his mind on what he should do and he always ended up saying, '*Okay, I will go out with her one more time and if it doesn't happen tonight, I'm going to back off,*' but even when it didn't happen he found himself still wanting to see her again. He missed talking to her when she wasn't around and although her plus size frame wasn't mind blowing; her beautiful face was such a pleasure to look at. Her conversation was always positive and interesting and he found himself wanting to be near her all the time.

"Yes I was, if that's alright with you," she said, answering his question.

He tried hard not to go there, but it was too late. He wanted this woman and it was nothing he could do to stop himself from wanting to be with her.

"Well give me five minutes to finish up one thing and then we can go so I can hear you sing a different tune for me," he said and kissed her passionately. She knew it was on. He couldn't deny it anymore he did want this woman. He wanted more than a date night stand in. He wanted to make her his woman.

"Okay," she whispered and smiled. He moved quickly and ran up the steps two by two to get to his office. He shut down his computer and gathered some paperwork and tossed it into his briefcase. He was just about to head to the door, but Johnson popped his head in. He and Johnson had known each other for years and he decided to bring him on as the new DJ at his club since the old DJ was not thrilled about working for a new boss and he quit.

"Hey, what's up Jay, you got a second?" he said, hating to impose on his time.

"Yea man, but that's all I got, I'm on my way out."

"Look man, I've been meaning to ask you," he said, beating around the bush.

"Yea dude, what's up?" he asked, trying to help him get to the point.

"You and Kennedy," he said, pausing. "I mean, are you actually seeing her now or are you still just kicking with her as a friend?" he asked curiously, going back to a conversation he had with Julian a few days ago. He had noticed Kennedy and she was definitely Johnson's type and he was kind of curious where they stood so he could holla at her.

"Why do you ask?" Julian said, feeling a little tension. He'd hoped his boy was not checking out his woman.

"Well the other day when we talked about it you said that she was just your friend and you wasn't feeling her like that, so I was just wondering you know, since she is single and we both know you don't get down like that with women like her."

"With women like her, what?" Julian asked, tilting his head and now with a little attitude.

"Come on Jay, you and I have been boys for years and I've never seen you kick it with a woman like Kennedy"

"What do you mean Jon? There's nothing wrong with Kennedy."

"Shit man, I know that, that sista is fine. I just know she is not your type."

"Oh so, why can't she be my type man?" he asked, putting his briefcase down.

"Look man," he said and paused for a second. He knew now that Julian liked Kennedy. He just didn't understand why just four, maybe five days ago he was saying, *'Dude, come on now, she is just cool people and I'm not feeling her like that. She and I are just friends, she is good people,'* he remembered him saying. "You know what? My bad brah, my bad okay. It's just that in all the honeys I've ever seen you kick it with; none were normal and regular like Kennedy. She is cool as hell and now I see that you feeling her. I know what time it is, so my bad," Johnson said, backing away to leave.

"Jon, you wanted to try to holla at her?" he asked.

"Naw man, I'm cool, it's just the other day you didn't seem too interested and now I see you are, so my bad," he said, trying to leave.

"Yo' Jon, I never said I wasn't feeling her."

"And you never said you were either. You said y'all just hanging as friends. That's what you said dude. Did I misunderstand?"

"Naw man, you didn't. That's what I thought, but man, this woman is," he said, then rolled his neck around as if he was trying to say she was getting to him. "Let's just say we more than friends, so don't even," he said letting Johnson know not to even attempt.

"I hear ya' dawg. You'd be a fool to let this one go," he said and turned to walk away.

"Well we'll see," Julian said softly and tuned out the light. He shut his office door and got a little jealous when he saw Kennedy sitting at the bar with Tony laughing it up and having what appeared to be a good ole time with him. *'Aw man, not him too'*, Julian thought to himself. He then realized that Kennedy was gorgeous and had an effect on men and most men were drawn to her exactly like he was.

"Baby, are you ready?" Julian asked interrupting the good time she and Tony was having.

"Yea, I'm ready," she said, turning around on her stool

giving him a warm, bright smile. He felt warm on the inside and when he smiled, she felt his energy and she could tell that he was ready to be with her that night.

"Listen Tony, I may not make it back tonight, but you can hit me on my cell if you need me…, only and only if it is an emergency," he stressed, making sure Tony understood that he didn't want to be disturbed.

"I got'cha Jay. We got it tonight, you have fun with your lady," he said and Julian smiled. '*My lady,*' he thought to himself. The idea wasn't so bad.

"Oh, I plan to," he said and helped Kennedy off the bar stool.

"Oh Tony listen, if you see my girls out here tonight, be sure to put their drinks on a tab for me and use this card," she said, trying to hand him a Visa. "Are you able to swipe it now for authorization and put their drinks on it?" she asked and Julian grabbed her hand.

"No, if you see her girls take care of them," he said and winked at Tony.

"Julian you don't have to, I'm good," she said, trying to give Tony the card again.

"No baby I'm good, now put your card back in your purse and Tony knows what to do," he said and Kennedy didn't fight. '*You gotta let a man be a man,*' she thought and smiled.

"Alright then," she said and slipped the card back into her purse. "I'll see you later, Tony."

"Okay, y'all take it easy," he said and continued to get the bar ready for the night.

Kennedy followed Julian outside and she decided it was best for her to follow him so she wouldn't have to leave her truck in the club's parking lot. She was smiling and couldn't wait to make it to his place. She was nervous and excited at the same time, because it had been so long since she had something inside of her and her body was already giving her signs of readiness. She noticed her nipples hardening through her shirt as she thought about it. She took a deep breath and calmed herself as she sat at the light behind him.

Chapter Eleven

She sat in her truck and counted to ten before she finally opened the door. Kennedy was more than ready to make it happen with Julian. The entire summer went by and they just talked, went to dinner and got in a movie here and there, so Kennedy couldn't comprehend it, but she knew for some reason Julian was holding back.

She'd linger around after the club in hopes he'd invite her to spend the night or stay at his place 'til after two in the morning sometimes, but a few kisses here and there was as far things would go. She knew he liked her and wasn't seeing anyone, but it was like he was hesitant in taking their relationship to a sexual, couple type relationship.

That night was different and she meant what she said when she told him that she wanted to sing for him, because she was ready and if even he didn't make a move, she was definitely going to make a move on him.

It was now or never she thought as she took her bath and dressed earlier that evening. She didn't know what to expect, so she was happy that he finally showed her sexual interest and the vibe she got from him at the club made her very aware that he was ready to break her off.

She got out and he was standing in the walkway next to his driveway waiting for her. They went inside and she took a seat on the sofa. She was nervous as hell and she didn't want it to show. She and Julian had grown close, so she felt safe and comfortable with him and didn't know why her hands wouldn't stop shaking. She excused herself to the bathroom and when she closed the door, she took a few deep breaths and stood still 'til the nervousness eased up and her hands were no longer shaking. She flushed and washed her hands even though she didn't go. She took another deep breath and went back and sat on the sofa.

"Would you like something to drink?" he asked, going over to the wet bar.

"Sure, I'll take a vodka and cranberry if you have it," she said. She usually asked for wine, but she was so nervous she needed something a bit stronger.

"Okay," he said and laughed.

"Why are you laughing?" she asked out of curiosity.

"Because you are nervous," he said and then proceeded to fix her drink.

"I am not," she said, lying.

"You are too, Kennedy. Since when do you drink vodka?" he asked, putting the ice cubes in the glass.

"Since forever, Julian," she said defensively. "And okay, I can't lie, I'm a little nervous," she said, telling him the truth.

"You don't have to be," he said. He walked over and handed her the glass.

"Thank you," she said softly and took a sip.

"You are welcome," he said, then sat next to her.

"You're not going to have anything?" she asked.

"Yea, in a moment," he said, looking at her. "You know, you have the most beautiful smile," he told her.

She blushed. "Really?" she asked.

"Yes, you do," he said and kissed her. The heat started to rise and she put her drink down.

"No baby, finish your drink," he said and stood. He went over to the bar and made himself a Crown on the rocks and came back to join her. They sat and didn't say much, just sipped their drinks. Kennedy was glad to have the vodka working into her system because she felt more relaxed.

"Listen, I'm going to go shower, do you want to join me?" he asked. Kennedy almost choked on her last swallow of vodka and cranberry. She coughed and he patted her back. "Baby, are you okay?" he asked as she tried to catch her breath.

"Yes..., yes..., yes," she said in between coughs. "You just caught me off guard."

"I see," he said, patting and rubbing her back, making sure she was okay.

"But I'm fine. I'm okay," she said, assuring him she was fine.

She wiped the tears from the corner of her eyes and he sat there for a moment or two for her to regain her poise. When she seemed ok, he stood and reached for her hand and she let him lead her into his master bedroom. He stopped to gently kiss her and she was mesmerized by him. He went into the master bath and started the water. She stood in one spot like she was afraid to move, so he moved over to her. He slowly began to undress her and then he undressed himself. He looked at her body and she being confident in who she was, stood there in her heels and matching lace panty and bra set she had gotten from the mall earlier that day. That confidence made him see her to be just as sexy as he wanted her to be.

He didn't know what to expect because he had never actually seen a plus size woman naked, so stretch marks and dimples were not what he was used to seeing, but she didn't look any less beautiful than he thought she would. He was tender to her as he would be to any woman and he gave her body just as much attention as he would have given to any other woman that he wanted.

They showered and he made sure he kissed and touched every inch of her. They pleased and teased each other with kisses and tongue movements, enough to practically lose their minds and decided it was time to get out of the shower and make what they had been dying to happen, happen. He handed her a nice and soft towel and wrapped his towel around his waist, then he went to get himself another drink. He came back and turned on the music and the confident and beautiful Kennedy was in his bed. He smile at her and was so ready to make her feel as good as the feeling she was giving to him.

He pulled the covers back and just looked at her. He was astonished how she carried herself with so much confidence. That, he never expected.

"What?" she asked, looking at him.

"Nothing, I just want to look at you," he said and she smiled.

"Well Julian, I'm ready to feel you," she said, then reached over and touched his erection.

"Aw baby, I am ready to feel you too," he said, breathing deeply.

"Well come here," she said. He climbed into bed with her and quickly took one of her ample breast into his mouth.

"Aw Julian," she moaned.

The heat from his wet mouth made her spot clench. She closed her eyes and couldn't help stroking his stiff dick. She was thanking God silently that he had something to work with. She just imagined how he would feel inside of her tight wetness. He positioned himself on top of her and he continued to massage and suck on her breast. The feeling was so good, it sent vibes to her tunnel and she automatically opened her legs wider. He got the hint that she was anxious, so he reached over and grabbed a condom from the top left night stand drawer.

She wondered if he had them on hand all the time, or if he had gotten them when they started dating. Either way, she was happy he thought to use one. There were times when she would be turned completely off by a man she had to ask to use one. She felt if they were just going to sleep with her without using anything, they did that shit with other women. She was happy to see that Julian had some type of sense. She knew he was a clean man and took care of himself. His home was immaculately clean all the time and he always smelled delicious, but STDs did not have an odor, nor could you see them on the service.

She relaxed and watched him open the wrapper and her clit jumped just watching him roll it on. She gave him an inviting smile and he came down on her, distracting her with his sensual kiss. His tongue ravished her mouth and she squealed when he forced himself inside of her. He was taken by the tight wetness her love nest gave him. They both were satisfied at the pleasure that their organs were experiencing. He didn't expect for her body to feel that good and she knew it would be good, but she didn't expect for it to be that good.

She turned her head to the side to not let him see the

expression on her face. He was making her insides sing and she moaned a sexy moan to let him know that he was giving her pleasure while he licked and sucked on her neck. He never had to concentrate on holding back, but he had to literally think about the music that was playing in the background to focus on something other than exploding after two minutes. It felt so good to him he wanted to kick himself for not making love to her sooner.

"Oh shit Kay baby, damn, girl…, aw shit baby," he said and she knew exactly where he was coming from.

"Is it good to you, baby?" she asked.

"Yes baby, you know it's good," he groaned.

"Tell me it's good," she said, turning to face him.

"It's good baby…, its good baby," he said in between kisses.

She grabbed the back of his head and they kissed deeply as he forced himself deeper inside of her body. It was feeling good to Kennedy, but the deeper he stroked her; it started hurt a little at the same time. She wanted him to ease up a little, but didn't want to stop him. Her cervix was not cooperating with the rest of her body and she knew she had to change positions before she had to stop.

"Baby, let me get on top," she said and he paused. He wondered if that was a good idea, but he was six feet, built and he was not afraid of her. He kissed her and eased out. He had to grab hold of the condom, because it was like her tightness wanted to hold on to it. He helped her to get in a comfortable position and he grabbed her ass and squeezed it. '*Lord have mercy,*' he thought to himself. He was used to dealing with skin and bones and Kennedy's body felt amazing on top of him. Her thickness was right and her loving was definitely right. No sharp limbs to stab him and her D cupped breasts softly brushed against his chest while she rode him.

"Aw baby, that shit is good," he groaned.

"You like that, baby?"

"Yes baby…, you are so damn good girl. Damn baby, damn. You want me to cum don't you?" he asked.

"You ready to cum daddy?" she asked, hoping the answer would be no.

"Shit girl, you working that shit right," he moaned,

impressed with her performance.

"You like that?" she asked him again.

"Yes baby. Is my dick good to you girl?" he asked, holding on to her ass and pumping the hell out of her. She was enjoying him, but he was sending his dick through the roof of her love nest and she knew that she was going to have girl problems.

"Yes..., yes...," she said, frowning. She was trying to hang in there, but it had been a while and Mr. Big Stuff wasn't taking it easy. Her body had to get used to him. "Hold on baby, wait..., wait..., wait," she said, easing up.

"What's wrong, baby?"

"Just give me a minute," she said, trying not to bitch up on him.

Ladies know when the cervix has issues there is no fun in love making. She laid on his chest and took deep breaths, hoping her body would not act up on her. She needed to wait a couple of moments before she could begin again.

"Are you alright?" he asked with concern.

"Yeah I'm fine. It's just been a while and it's just a little painful," she said, telling him the truth.

"We can take it slow," he said, kissing her cheek.

He wanted to get back to what they were doing because her loving was unbelievably good and he knew that he wasn't going to allow another man an opportunity to experience her body again. He was done for sure with any thoughts of not being with Kennedy. She had all the qualities that he wanted in a woman and to top it off, she had some good loving. That was like the cherry on top. No way could he have found smart, funny, successful and good pussy. It was like he hit the jack pot and to think he avoided his feelings and tried to hide from love.

He didn't know what had come over him or what had happened that quickly, but he knew Kennedy was the woman he wanted to be with.

"Baby, you want to take it slow?" he asked, gently caressing her back.

"Yes," she whispered and began to roll her hips.

He didn't push back; he just let her do her thang. He tried to fight the urge of shooting hot shit into the plastic, but her body and her kisses were just too much for him, so he squeezed her tight and let it go. He groaned, moaned and grasp for air as he held onto her. She was happy that he had climaxed because she wasn't sure how much more she could take and hated that she had the awful pain going on in her stomach.

She stayed on top of him for a while and let him caress her back. She gave him a couple soft kisses to show him that she enjoyed him as much as he enjoyed her. She finally moved and he got up and went into the bathroom. She heard him flush the condom and he came back and climbed back into bed with her. He wrapped himself around her plump body. He smiled because he now understood what men meant by saying having something to hold on to.

"Are you okay baby?" he whispered in her ear.

"I'm perfect," she replied.

"That you are," he said and she smiled. "Are you going to give me some more?" he asked and she felt his dick enlarging on her ass.

"Only if you be gentle," she said. She felt like she was failing miserably for their first time. She was a wild one in bed, but her body was rusty and her mechanics were malfunctioning.

"Yea baby, I'll be as gentle as you want me to be," he said, reaching into his drawer to get another piece of plastic.

"Okay baby," she said and it was on again.

To her surprise, it was better that time because he gently rolled around inside of her and allowed her to have an orgasm out of this world. She fell asleep so fast after they were done, that she didn't hear him flush the second condom.

Chapter Twelve

Kennedy eased out of bed trying not to wake him. She looked over at the clock and she had to get up because there was no more snooze time left and if she didn't get a move on, she would definitely not make it to the store on time. She had been seeing Julian for over a year and there had been so many mornings she had called Teresa to open for her. She knew she was wearing out her welcome with Teresa and she was trying to break that habit. Not that Teresa complained or anything, but she didn't want to take advantage of her. She herself had a man now and she managed to cover her own opening shifts, so Kennedy being the owner, had to do the same.

She just hated time away from Julian, she had to be close to him every opportunity she could. Now that she had suggested changes for the club, he was busier and they had more late nights than ever. During the day, he'd be at one of his restaurants and now that he had the club going five nights a week, he was always busy.

Friday and Saturday nights were the normal club nights, Sundays were old school Sundays, Mondays were blue Mondays where they played the blues and thanks to Kennedy letting her singing ability out of the bag, Wednesdays was Karaoke night, so they were always busy and always at the club. Kennedy was happy and Julian made her happy. She would be tired as hell, but she still was there when he wanted her there. She didn't understand why she was still getting dirty looks after so long from women, but she learned early to not let it get to her.

She trusted Julian and mostly everyone knew that she was

his woman, but on occasion, there would be one or two new ones that were in his face, or the bold ones who just didn't give a damn to make passes or deliberately flirt with him in front of her face. She used to be pissed and keep an attitude 'til one night Julian had to tell her, "Listen, baby, it's the business and you are the only woman for me. You can't keep trippin' out on me when someone says something to me. If I was on some bullshit, I wouldn't have you here with me every time the club is open. You gotta trust me babe." After that, she started to relax.

She showered and moved around her room quietly. She pushed her bathroom door closed and applied her make-up to keep the light from bothering him. He had worked at the club the night before and got to her a little later than usual, so she knew he was tired. She was at the club as well, but left before it got too late because she was tired.

She tried to wait up for him and that was a losing battle, but she didn't hesitate to get up when he eased into bed and give him some late night loving. Since his nights were sometimes late, she gave him a key so she wouldn't have to get up and go downstairs to let him in. She made it clear that he didn't have the freedom to just walk in whenever he wanted to; she just needed a way to not have to get up all the time when she was in a deep sleep.

She smiled at him sleeping so peacefully. He was a hard working man and every piece of wealth he had, he surely earned it, so she admired him and her daddy loved him. Everybody thought he was a great guy but Cher. For some reason, she always frowned on him and never really cared too much for him. Kennedy didn't know why because she was with Cortez, so she couldn't have been jealous. She just couldn't figure out why Cher was like that with him.

Teresa loved him, her cousins approved of him, but what Cher's problem was, she didn't know and it had gotten to the point of Kennedy not even caring. She stop asking Julian what was up with her, because Julian didn't care for Cher, so all they did was talk shit to each other. Kennedy just summed it up like *Martin and Pam* from the *Martin* sitcom. She just let them hate each other.

She was ready for work, it was time to go and she didn't want to disturb him, but she had to kiss him goodbye.

"You're leaving already, babe?" he asked when he felt her kiss.

"Yeah, I am running a little late this morning," she said.

"Oh okay. Call me and wake me by one. I have to head over to one of the restaurants when I leave here."

"Okay, now get some sleep baby. I love you," she said and kissed him again.

"Okay baby, have a good morning and I love you too," he said and turned over.

He was used to staying at Kennedy's because he usually came to her place after the club since she had to start her mornings earlier than he did. He had a little drawer space and she created a corner in her tight closet for a few of his items and shoes. They were seriously seeing each other and they spent a lot of time together.

"Hey put something on, Julian is here," Kennedy, told Cherae who was in the kitchen half dressed as usual.

"He's always here," she barked.

"And this is my house Cher," Kennedy said, taking her coat from the coat closet.

"I know this is your house Kay. Must you remind me every other day?" she asked, slamming the fridge.

"Listen Cher, I'm sorry okay. I am not trying to throw it in your face, but I have asked you so many times to put clothes on. Julian is here a lot because he is my man and the way our hours are it is more convenient for him to come here. All I ask you to do is try to cover yourself up Cher. I don't walk around half dressed because I know I share this place with you and I would like you to keep in mind that you share this space with me. Would you want Cortez to see me in skimpy pajamas and lingerie?" she asked, trying to make her girl get a clue.

"Fine Kay, I will put something on," she said and stormed out of the kitchen. *'Cortez wouldn't look at your fat ass anyway, even if you walked around naked,'* Cher said under her breath softly as she stormed into her room.

Kennedy was getting so tired of her; it was like telling a child to do something over and over again. Kennedy wanted to go behind her, but she had to get to work and didn't have time to fuss with Cher. She grabbed her keys and headed out the door.

She drove to work and made it just in time to open the store on time. She was happy when more of her staff started to come in. She hated being at the store alone, but in the early morning hours, no one came in the store and even though they opened at ten, the next person didn't come in 'til eleven.

When Teresa got there at twelve, she was happy to see her because she had realized she left without her cell phone that morning and she had to run home to get it. She was smiling because she could have the opportunity to wake Julian up at one in person.

"Hey girl, I'm glad you are here. Listen, I have to run home in a few, because I forgot my cell phone this morning, but I'll be back.

"Okay that's fine," Teresa said.

After she finished up the stores time sheets, she headed home. She got to her house and realized Cher's car was still there. She thought to herself, *'Why is this heifer not at work?'* She parked in the driveway and she got a funny feeling in the pit of her stomach. She got out and walked up the steps of the porch and wondered what her excuse would be this time for not going into work. When she opened the door, the house was quiet.

"Cher?" she called out as she locked the door. "Cher?" she called again and nothing. She went down the hall to Cher's room and stood on the outside of her door and said her name again, but she didn't respond. She pushed the door open and Cher was not in her room. Instantly, she ran up the stairs and almost broke the door off the hinge when she pushed it open. Julian jumped up out of his sleep and looked at her like *'what in the hell.'*

"Baby, what..., what is it?" he asked as she went into her bathroom. She knew that bitch was up in her room somewhere. "Baby, what's wrong with you?" he asked when she snatched the closet door open and Cher was not there either. "Kennedy, baby, what the fuck are you doing?" he asked, getting up out of the bed. His dick was hanging because that was how Kennedy left him that morning in her bed, naked.

She calmed down and didn't say anything to Julian about what she was thinking. "My phone, I left my phone this morning and I don't know where it is," she said lying, something she vowed she'd never do under any circumstances. She felt foolish for thinking Cher would be in her room, fucking her man under her roof.

"It's over here baby," he said, going over to her nightstand.

"Thank you Jay," she said, calming down. "I don't know what I was thinking. I came home because I thought I lost it somewhere," she said and paused. "I don't know what I was thinking," she said, trying to act natural. "Look babe, I gotta get back to the store. Are you good, it's close to one?" she said, confused and feeling foolish for the thought she had in her head about her man and best friend.

"Baby I'm good. I'm going to get ready now," he said, reaching for his boxers that were on the floor and stepping into them.

"Okay baby, I'm gone. I will see you later tonight," she said and gave him another kiss.

"Are you sure you are okay?" he asked.

"Yeah I'm good," she said, still not able to digest that feeling she had in the pit of her stomach.

"Come on, I'll walk you to the door," he said, taking her by the hand.

"Okay," she said and they walked out the room.

She walked down the steps wondering where Cher was without her car and then she figured maybe Cortez had picked her up. She didn't beat her brain about it, she just let it go.

"You gon' meet me at the club?"

"Yea, I'll be there by 7:00 or 7:30," she said.

"Okay baby. I love you, see you later."

"I love you too," she said and he shut the door behind her.

She walked down the porch feeling foolish and was glad she didn't walk in on what she thought she was walking in on. She started her truck and pulled out of her driveway and then she immediately called Teresa to tell her what just happened.

Chapter Thirteen

"Is she gone?" Cher whispered when Julian came back into Kennedy's room.

"Yea, she's gone," he said.

She crawled out of the tight corner behind Kennedy's chair and ottoman. How she managed to fit back there neither one of them knew, but when they heard Kennedy's voice from the main floor, they panicked. She knew the bathroom and the closet was a no, no, so she squeezed into the tiny opening behind Kennedy's chair and squatted down as low as she could. She was sweating bullets behind the chair, hoping Kennedy wouldn't see her.

"Are you outta your mind Cherae?" he asked angrily.

"What?" she asked, just as clueless as hell.

"What in the fuck do you mean..., 'what'?" he yelled, looking at her like she was crazy. She was dumber than a sack of rocks he thought to himself, thinking about the mess she pulled. "Why did you come up here in the first place?" Julian continued, yelling at her while he quickly put on his clothes. He was only interested in getting the hell out of there and away from her.

"Because I'm tired of you playing games with me Julian. You know you want me Jay, so why are you acting like you don't?" she asked, crawling across Kennedy's king size bed trying to get to him. She got on her knees and tried to undo the buttons he had buttoned while he was trying to dress as quickly as possible.

"Get your hands off me," he snapped, then knocked her hands away. "I told you once, twice, one hundred times before that I don't want you. I'm in love with Kennedy, Cherae and I've told you from day one, that you and I will never hook up. I don't want you."

"Yeah, whatever..., you know you wanna fuck me, Julian. You just scared that Kennedy will find out and see you for who you really are. I told you, I'll never tell her. I wouldn't do that," she said and he was wondering was she really as crazy as she was acting.

"Unbelievable..., you are twisted as fuck, you know that, Cherae? And if you keep this bullshit up I promise you I will tell Kennedy on yo' ass."

"Tell Kennedy what? How you let me suck yo' dick, right here in this bed last year? Right here in her bed?"

"Oh, you are on that bullshit again? Cherae you know I didn't know it was you," he said.

"Come on Julian, you knew it was me. No way can you tell me that you didn't know it was me. That is a lie you can save for your woman, because I ain't buying it."

"No, I didn't know it was you because I was half asleep and had Crown in me. You came up here in the middle of the night and it was pitch black. I woke up to you sucking my dick. It took me what, less than thirty seconds to realize it was you? Any sane bitch would have gotten the hint and given up after a man damn near tossed her ass to the other side of the room."

"Don't even try it Julian, you know you enjoyed it. You didn't push me off 'til your dick got ready to explode inside of my mouth, so now what?" she asked with her own twisted version of how things went down.

The night it happened they had all gone out and Teresa had too much to drink, so Kennedy had to drive her home. She asked Julian to give Cherae a ride back to the house while she made sure Teresa got home safely. Not wanting to, he agreed to let the evil one ride with him. He hated to be anywhere near Cherae without Kennedy being around because she constantly flirted and fucked with him.

When they got to the house, Julian went upstairs as quickly as he could, after refusing Cher's advances again on the staircase and closed the door. He undressed and climbed into bed in hopes to have Kennedy on top of him soon, but he dosed off waiting for her.

When Kennedy got to Teresa's house, Teresa got sick and threw up everywhere and Kennedy being her friend, had to stay longer to clean her up and get her to bed and to clean up the mess she had made in the bathroom. She tried to call Julian to tell him that she was going to be there for a while, but he was sleep and his cell phone was in his pants pocket. She then called Cherae just so they wouldn't worry about her and that's when Cherae crept up the steps and eased into bed with Julian. The room was dark and he was in a deep sleep, so she pulled the covers back and took him inside of her mouth.

He felt her mouth, but he thought it was Kennedy, so he just laid there with his eyes closed and allowed her to suck his dick. He didn't realize it was not Kennedy until he reached to touch her ass and realized it was not Kennedy's ass. His eyes popped open wide and he tried to focus them in the dark, but automatically knew it was Cherae. He jumped up, backed away and ordered her to leave, but she came close and tried to kiss him. He damn near tossed her ass into the master bathroom as hard as he pushed her to get off of him. He was mad as hell and he couldn't believe that Cher had gotten that bold and in Kennedy's bed.

They got into it and exchanged words and he threatened he would tell Kennedy. He wished he had because now things were too out of hand and Cherae was just walking around like she was the shit. That made him want to tell Kennedy so he would not have to worry about being around her ass ever again, but he was sure that Kennedy wouldn't believe him if he did tell her what Cherae was up to.

"Look Cherae, you need to stay the fuck away from me. You got that? I'm not gon' tell you again. I am not interested in you and I have no intentions of ever, ever being with you. Kennedy is who I love and who I want, so you need to chill the fuck out."

"Why Julian? Kennedy doesn't have to know. Please baby, please..., I just want you so bad and I wanna feel that big dick. I know you wanna fuck me Julian. I see how you look at me and I know you want me," she said desperately. She tried to hug his neck and he stepped back from her embrace.

"Cherae what's wrong with you? Do you hate Kennedy that

much? Why would you want to do that to her? Why would you do that to your friend, Cherae?"

"I don't hate Kennedy, Julian. I love her; she is like a sister to me. I don't want to hurt her. I just want you, why can't you understand that? It's not about her, it's about you," she said, trying to move closer to him. He steadily backed away.

"If Kennedy is like a sister to you Cherae, what kinda friend are you to her to want to go behind her back and fuck with her man?"

"You don't understand Julian," she snapped. He thought boy she is a live one.

"Understand what, Cherae? What am I supposed to be trying to understand? What did Kennedy do so horrible to you to make you want me so bad?"

"Again, since you were not listening. This ain't about Kennedy. That night we met I know you wanted me. You stood between me and Kennedy and I saw the way you were looking at me, but you didn't holla at me. Why you didn't had me confused and then you hook up with Kennedy over me?" she said, looking at him like, '*how could you look over me and want her.*'

"Oh, so that's what it is? Since your ego is bruised you are out to prove that you are the bomb and Kennedy is just…, what?"

"Not me," she barked.

"Look Cherae, I don't know what type of jealous or crazy issues you got going on, but I am with Kennedy. That is my woman, that is the woman I want to be with and I'm sorry, but I wouldn't hurt her like that, so please give it a rest. You and I will never, ever be in any type of situation like this again. You got that?"

"Julian please," she said with her eyes welling and he just looked at her. "If you don't fuck me the way I know you wanna fuck me," she said, laying back on the bed and spreading her legs. "I'm gon' tell her," she threatened.

"No you're not Cherae. If you wanted to tell her, you would have told her. You would have never squeezed your scary ass behind that chair when you heard her come in. I'm not worried about you Cherae and you can open your legs for the next man, because I still don't want it," he said and turned and walked out.

He left her there on Kennedy's bed looking crazy with her legs wide open. She was hurt and furious and she knew she was going have to do something to make Julian see that she wasn't going to give up. Eventually, he was going to give in to her. She was going to show him that he should have chosen her from the very beginning. No way was Kennedy just going to have it all. She came from a family with everything. Money, wealth and she never had to struggle for anything. She was smart and had everything she wanted.

Cherae was tired of having to fuck men to get anything. Kennedy was an overweight bitch and had a fine ass wealthy man and all Cherae had was an old ass Honda Civic that was falling apart by the month since she had made her final payment on it. She was stuck in a dead end job at the telephone company that she hated. She had barely enough money in the bank to fill up her gas tank. She and Cortez were dating, but she didn't want him like she wanted Julian. She started to hate to see Julian and Kennedy together.

She hated that they could go and do whatever they wanted and she still had to fuck old men on the side just to maintain her diva lifestyle of shopping and fronting. She felt like she was too beautiful to not have what she wanted. Even Teresa and her man were still together and talking marriage and where was she? Everyone had a life and something good going on but her. Her girls were moving forward and growing in love and life and she was stuck in a rut. She had no idea what she was going to do with the rest of her life and she didn't know why she was so jealous of Kennedy.

Chapter Fourteen

"You're coming over tonight after you're done?" Kennedy asked Julian and he didn't hear her. He was trying to concentrate on his paperwork and trying to get the image of Cher's neatly trimmed pussy out of his mind. He knew it was wrong, but his dick kept reminding him of how sexy and firm her body was. She was a dime and his boys would think he was stupid not to want her. She was gorgeous, but she was still his woman's best friend. "Baby, are you coming by when you leave here tonight?" she asked him. He looked up at her.

"Huh baby? I'm sorry, what did you ask me?" he replied.

"Are you okay Julian? You've been acting weird all day today and you are like in another world tonight," she said. He tried to come back to normal.

"I'm sorry babe. I'm just swamped with this paperwork. I'm trying to get caught up with the books for the restaurants and the club, I'm just a little behind baby," he said, trying to reassure her that he was fine.

"Is there something I can help you with?" she asked, sitting down on the opposite end of the table where he was sitting.

"No babe, I got it. You gon' home and I will be there after we close."

"Okay," she said, standing to leave. "Are you sure that is all that is bothering you?"

"Yea babe, I'm cool. I will finish up here and I will be back to my normal self by the time I get there tonight.

"Okay baby, I'll see you. I love you," she said sweetly and he knew she did. She kissed him on the lips and got her things to go. "See ya, Tony," she said as she walked passed the bar.

"Later Ms. Kennedy," he said, placing a customer's drink on the bar.

Kennedy got in her truck and still felt a little funny about earlier, but she just let it go. She drove home wondering what Cher had planned for the night. She normally came to the club, but she hadn't showed up before Kennedy left. When she got in she called her name, but she didn't respond.

"Cher?" Kennedy called out again. She came out in a little, cute dress, showing off her everything.

"Hey," she said, walking over to her mirrored wall in the living room to check herself out.

"Wow sexy momma, you and Cortez got a date?" Kennedy asked, checking her out. She was looking good that night and Kennedy had to compliment her. "You're looking good girl," she said.

"Naw, I'm headed over to Jay's for a little bit. I thought you'd still be there."

"Girl, I am tired and I thought I had a headache coming on, but I feel better now."

"Okay then, I'm gone," she said, taking her purse off the sofa and headed for the door.

"Oh Cher, did you go to work today?"

"Yea, why?"

"Well I came home today a little after twelve and your car was still here," she said curiously.

"Cortez picked me up and took me to breakfast and then he dropped me off at work," she said, quickly coming up with a lie.

"Oh okay," Kennedy said, dismissing it. She knew that funny feeling was for nothing.

"Well I got to run," she said so she could get away from more of Kennedy's questions.

She hadn't gone to work at all that day. She called in as soon as Kennedy said Julian was there. After she made sure Kennedy was gone, she took a nice long shower, fixed her hair and made her face and eased right on up the stairs to join Julian in Kennedy's bed.

When she eased in bed with him, she pulled the covers

back and she was even more excited when she saw him naked. She took his dick inside of her mouth and he jumped out of his sleep. It was early in the day, so he knew it was Cherae and he yelled at her while trying to stop her, but she had a good hold on it and a grip on his balls. He calmed down and tried to talk calmly to her and begged her to stop, but she continued. He couldn't concentrate or even enjoy it because he didn't want to be in that type of situation.

He couldn't take it anymore so he decided he'd just yank her ass off by the hair, even if he hurt himself in the process, but then they heard Kennedy's voice calling out for Cher. They both froze and Julian was scared because that was a bad scene and even though he was innocent, he'd look guilty as hell. They both panicked, but quick and scary ass Cher got up and squeezed her tiny ass in the corner behind the chair. He heard Kennedy coming up the steps so he pulled the covers up, closed his eyes and prayed to God that she would not see Cher's naked ass behind the chair.

He was so happy to get Kennedy down the stairs and out of the house without seeing her trifling friend in her room balled up behind her chair butt ass naked. She would have beaten the dog shit out of Cher and he knew that would have been the end for him too. He went back up the steps and found Cherae sweating bullets.

"Well let me call Julian and let him know you're on your way," Kennedy said and Cherae stopped in her tracks.

"No, no, no…., you don't have to call him," she said, coming back toward the kitchen where Kennedy headed to get the cordless.

"Why not, do you want to pay to get in?"

"Yea, I mean, I'm good. Cortez is gonna meet me there. So, I'm good," she said nervously. She didn't want to alert Julian that she was coming because she didn't want him to leave before she got there. She was looking fabulous and Kennedy wasn't going to be there either. That was too perfect.

"Okay Cher, suit yourself. When you see him, tell him momma said don't keep me waiting long," she said, putting her hands on her hips.

"Okay I will," Cherae said, thinking, '*whatever, I ain't telling him shit, big momma.*'

She raced to the door and quickly hopped in her car. She

drove down the streets singing and feeling good. She had plans that night and it wasn't with Cortez. She had only one thing and one man on her mind. '*I'm going to walk up on him and demand that he fuck me at once,*' she said to herself and laughed out loud as she parked in the spot next to his Mercedes. That was the spot Kennedy parked her Denali in. *"Kennedy ain't here, is she?"* Cher said as she whipped her Honda into the stall.

She turned off the engine and pulled her visor down to check the mirror again. Since Kennedy was the generous one and bought Cherae the same things she bought for herself, her make-up was flawless because it was the good shit, not that Walgreen's type mess that Cherae used to buy before Kennedy started buying make-up for her. She admired how good she was looking and closed the visor. She took her smell good out of her purse and gave her hot spots another squirt and got out of the car.

The guy at the door was familiar with her and let her in free anyway and she headed straight for the bar.

"Hey, hey, beautiful, what's going on?" Tony asked.

"Hey Mr. Tony, what's good?"

"Nothing too much, what you drinking?" he asked and placed a napkin in front of her.

"A double Henney on the rocks with a splash of Coke."

"Okay, got that coming up for you," he said and went to make her drink. She looked around to see if she could spot him, but she didn't. She knew he was still there because his car was out front, so she decided she'd just ask Tony.

"Thanks," she said, going into her purse when he put her drink down.

"No baby, it's on the house," he said and she was relieved. All she had was twenty dollars and she had to put gas in her car because her tank was on empty. It was Monday and she wasn't going to get a check 'til that Friday, so she thanked God she didn't have to pay for her drink.

"Thanks Tony. Where's your boss? I wanna holla at him," she asked.

"Up in his office," he said, pointing at the stairs.

"Okay, I'll see you. I need to go take care of something," she said and hurried across the room. Julian's office was up a spiral staircase that always had a sign in front of it that read employees only. Cherae eased past the sign and walked up the steps. She took a swallow of her drink and straightened herself and then tapped on the door softly.

"Yea," she heard Julian answer and then she tapped again. She didn't want to say who it was, so she opened the door. He had his eyes on the monitor and was shocked to see her when he looked up. "Cherae, what are you doing?" he asked.

"Hello Julian," she said seductively.

"Cherae," he said looking at her strangely.

"I came to see you Jay," she said and moved closer to his desk.

He scooted his chair back from under the desk and stood up. "Listen Cherae, I've asked you to stay away from me, so why are you here?' he asked.

She walked around and got up in his face. "Because you and I got some unfinished business to take care of," she said. She sat her drink and purse on his desk.

"What unfinished business? What are you talking about?" he asked, backing up. She was right in front of him and he knew that he needed space between them.

"Look Julian, I'm not fucking around. Now, you're gonna fuck me. You're gonna please my pussy the way I want you to, so why don't you cut out this bullshit and just do it?" she told him. Julian was starting to lose his patience with her, but it was no stopping Cherae. "Now, you know that I'm what you want and no way can you not want to put your dick up in me. There is no way you don't find me sexy," she said, letting her dress hit the floor.

"You're out of your mind Cherae. You are one fucked up sista," he said, trying not to look at her perky tits and tight, flat stomach.

"I'm not crazy Julian. You are the one that is crazy. Only a crazy man would look at me," she said, sliding her thong down her thighs. "And not want me." She stood there in a pair of leather boots and thigh highs. She was sexy as hell and looked so good to him, but Julian was a smart man and he knew to leave.

"Cher, put your clothes back on," he demanded, trying so hard not to look at her, but her breasts were perfect and her skin looked so smooth and pretty. Her high yellow complexion was blemish free he thought to himself, looking at her frame. Her body was sexy and Cherae was model sexy no doubt, but she was his woman's best friend and he couldn't do it.

"Why are you fighting this? Look at me, I can tell you like what you see. All you got to do is relax baby and let me make you feel good," she said, now standing in front of him. Her nipples were so close they were touching his chest.

"Look," he said after snapping back to reality. For a moment he saw himself grabbing her. Throwing her on his desk and fucking her like she wanted him to and holding the back of Cher's head while he pushed his dick down her throat. "I'm going downstairs and when I get back I want you gone," he said and walked away, leaving her standing there. The aroma of her perfume filled his office and he was grateful to make it to the other side of the door without doing the unthinkable with her.

She was furious with Julian. How could he just walk away and leave her standing there? She was throwing herself at him, pulling out all of her tricks and he wasn't falling for it. "Oh no," she said as she put on her clothes. The tears started to burn her eyes and she wanted to do something to hurt him the way he had hurt her. She knew in her heart that he wanted her and didn't understand what Kennedy had done to him to make him want her fat ass more than he wanted her.

Julian went straight to the men's room and splashed cold water in his face. He was so mad at himself for what he was feeling. He couldn't believe that he had a moment when he wanted to fuck the shit out of Cher. He was so mad that she was doing that shit to him and he knew he had to get out of there quick. His dick was still hard and he decided to leave and go to Kennedy before he went back upstairs and did things to Cher that he knew she wanted him to do. He dried his face and headed for the door. He had to get to his woman and give her some of the good loving that Cher wanted him to give to her.

Chapter Fifteen

When Cher finally made it home, she saw Julian's car and she wanted to key it. She went inside and thought about marching up the steps and telling Kennedy that her man was sleeping with her too, but where would she go after Kennedy kicked her out? She went into her bathroom, undressed and took a shower. She brushed her teeth wondering what she could do to make him pay for what he was doing to her, but she couldn't come up with anything.

She wrapped her towel around her body and when she got in her room she tossed it onto her bench that sat at the foot of her bed. She climbed into bed and she felt his warm body and she jumped.

"Shhh," he said and whispered. "This is what you wanted?" She smiled and let him kiss her. He found his way to her nipples and sucked them so hungrily she wanted to scream. She moaned as softly as she could, not wanting Kennedy to hear, but he felt so damn good, she couldn't contain herself.

"Aw Julian, aw baby, yeah that's it right there," Cherae moaned. "Ooh yeah baby, that is so good, baby give it to me," Cherae said and rubbed the back of his head. She closed her eyes and allowed him to give her all of him. She was so happy to finally have him in her bed and between her legs.

"Oh Cherae, your shit is good baby," he whispered in her ear. He pushed deeper inside of her and she enjoyed every moment. "You gon' make me burst baby," he said.

She rolled her hips to help him. "Come on baby give me that sweet shit," she said, exciting him even more. They both were in ecstasy and Cherae knew that was what he wanted from the start. "I told you, you were gonna love this daddy."

"I do baby, I do," he said, breathing in her ear.

"Say my name," she begged.

"Cherae..., Cherae," he sang for her.

Her body went numb. She began to orgasm and he could feel the moisture from her exploding all over his dick. Since this wasn't planned, he fucked her without the plastic. He squeezed her tight when he released all of his juices inside of her and Cherae was more than satisfied with his performance. They kissed deeply and she was elated that she had finally convinced him to give her what she knew they both wanted. She had plans to make him her man and however she and Kennedy ended up was not her concern.

"Are you ready for round two?" he asked her.

She was just about to say, "Oh yes, baby," and then the ringing phone woke her up from her dream. She jumped up and looked around and didn't believe it was only a dream. Julian was not in her bed and she had not accomplished her mission to have him. She gathered her thoughts and by then, she missed a call from Cortez. She wondered why he called so late. It was 2:47 a.m. and she wondered what he needed at that time of morning.

She liked Cortez, but she loved Julian. She thought Cortez was good looking and he was definitely a catch, but he wasn't good in bed. After a year of sleeping with him, he was still a minute man. He could lick her to paradise, but after that, when she was ready for the thunder, he couldn't bring it. What she hated the most was he had a big dick. A big beautiful one, but it was useless because as soon as it got close to being the bomb, he'd explode.

So they were on and off. She loved being with him and loved the jealous looks and stares that she got from other women. They were both good looking people and they looked good when they were out together. She loved being the focus of men and women, hell; it didn't matter as long as all eyes were on her.

She got up and went to the bathroom. Since her room was one of four spare rooms. She didn't have the luxury of having a bathroom in her room like Kennedy, but since they had a small bathroom off the kitchen, she had the hall bathroom that was near her bedroom all to herself. When she was going back to her room, she heard moaning and she stopped in her tracks. As long as she lived with Kennedy and as long as Kennedy had been with Julian she had never overheard them making love. She stood still for a moment and from the moans that Kennedy made, Cherae figured that Julian was getting the job done.

The sound drew her closer to the steps and she continued to listen. Cher, unable to resist, tiptoed up the steps and stood outside of the door to listen to them. Her obsession with Julian was what made her courageous enough to even climb the steps. She closed her eyes and listened to Kennedy moan from the pleasure that Julian was giving her and Cherae wished that it was her he was giving his loving to.

When she heard Julian's voice groaning too, her spot got wet. She was almost tempted to touch herself until she heard Julian say, '*Kennedy baby, aw Kennedy, I'm cumin.*' She snapped out of it. He was with Kennedy and he was Kennedy's man and no matter how many tricks she came up with, he still wanted Kennedy.

She eased down the stairs and went back to her room. She was so hot and horny. When she got in her bed it was difficult for her to fall asleep. She looked at the clock and it was 3:05 a.m., so she grabbed her cell phone and called Cortez.

"Hey babe," he said, answering on the third ring.

"Hey you tried to call me?"

"Yeah, I just left this spot with one of my guys and it was on your end so I wanted to try and come through to see you, but I'm on the expressway now."

"Well how far are you?"

"Not far," he said, exiting. He already knew what she was going to say next.

"So, why don't you turn around and come back?" she asked.

"Okay, give me fifteen or twenty and I'll be there," he said.

"Okay babe." She hung up and went into the bathroom again to freshen up and brush her teeth. When she came out of the bathroom she heard someone in the kitchen and she was happy to see it was Julian. "Hey," she said to him and he didn't turn around.

"Hey," he said, taking a bowl from the cabinet. He grabbed two spoons and the scooper from the drawer and went into the freezer and got the ice cream.

"Ooh, ice cream is my favorite," Cherae said, coming into the kitchen.

"Yea, its Kennedy's favorite too," he said, reminding her that he was there for Kennedy and Kennedy only.

"Yes, as if I didn't know that. We've only been friends since we were seven," she said, getting smart.

"Since you were seven, huh?" he asked, piling the ice cream in the bowl.

"Yea and?"

"That's a long time to be friends with someone and want to stab them in the back," he said, putting the lid back on the container.

Cher was about to say something else smart, but there was a knock on the door. She knew it was Cortez and he was smart enough to tap and not ring the bell at that hour. She looked a Julian with an evil look and then walked away.

Cher went to let Cortez in and Julian was on his way upstairs. They met before he got to the steps.

"Hey Julian, what's going on?" Cortez said and Julian put the two spoons in the bowl to shake hands.

"Nothing too much man. My girl gotta have the ice cream," he said.

"Yeah man, I hear ya, but I see two spoons," he joked.

"Yeah, you know how it is. If I didn't get my own spoon she'd feed it to me anyway."

"I know that's real," he said.

"Well I'll holla at you man," Julian said, trying to make his way back up the steps.

"Al'ight man," Cortez said and Julian was off.

Cherae had already gone into her room because she didn't want to stand around to listen to them chat. She was in her bed naked when Cortez came in. She had plans to give her porn star performance that night. She had every intention to be as loud as she could because she wanted Julian to hear her. She figured if he heard her how good she was, he'd fantasize about her the way she fantasized about him.

She and Cortez got going and all the while she closed her eyes and imagined it was Julian. She was surprised and pleased that Cortez lasted longer than he normally did and she didn't have to act so much because that night it was really good. When they were done, she laid with a smile, not because it was good, but she had it in her mind that Julian overheard them and it was making him want her. She kissed Cortez, rested on his chest and fell asleep with the image of Julian in her head.

Chapter Sixteen

The next morning, Kennedy was in the kitchen cooking breakfast in a fantastic mood. She had the music on and the window was cracked, allowing a crisp September breeze in. She was singing along with the music and Julian came in the kitchen.

"Sing baby, sing it," he said, coming up behind her.

"Good morning baby," she said.

"Don't you mean good afternoon?" he asked, bringing her attention to the clock on the microwave because it was a quarter 'til one.

"Yeah, my bad," she said, cracking an egg. He leaned over and gave her a kiss and then reached for her glass of orange juice that was next to her on the counter.

"Hey, get your own," she said playfully, taking her glass out of his hand.

"Good morning," Cherae said.

"Morn...," Kennedy was about to say 'til she turned and saw Cher in a little tee shirt gown that barely covered the bottom of her yellow ass cheeks. "Cher," she said, putting down the wisp. She was getting ready to beat the eggs with it, but after seeing Cher, she was ready to beat Cher's ass with it.

"What?" she asked with attitude and a frown on her face.

"We need to talk," Kennedy said, walking by her. "Now," she said firmly.

Cherae knew that meant follow me. She blew out some air and slammed the juice container she had just taken out of the fridge on the island and followed Kennedy into the dining room.

"What now?" Cherae asked like she was agitated.

"What do you think? You knew Julian came over last night and you bring your ass into the kitchen like he ain't here," Kennedy said, trying not to be loud.

"Kay, I did not know he was still here," she said, lying to Kennedy's face and Kennedy knew it.

"That's bullshit Cherae. You know what?" Kennedy said, putting her hand over her head. She was getting so sick of Cher's attitude. "The thing is, you don't have respect for anybody, not even yourself. You don't respect me, you don't respect my house and you have absolutely no respect for my relationship," Kennedy said. She knew her words were useless.

"Your house, your this and your that. That is all you talk about Kennedy Renee and I'm getting tired of hearing it. I'm getting tired of hearing how this is your fucking house and furthermore, why don't you tell your man to keep his eyes off me since I'm the problem."

"Cher are you outta your damn mind? You think you are not the problem? You think you can walk around here half naked in front of my man and he is just supposed to keep his eyes off you? Is that what you think? Use your head for once and act like God put a brain underneath that pretty scalp of yours. This conversation is about you simply putting on some damn clothes Cherae. And I don't want to constantly remind you that this is my house, but I want you to show respect in this house. Give me the same respect I give you. You don't see me walking around half dressed in front of Cortez."

"Look Kay, like I said, I didn't know he was still here," she said, turning her head, not wanting to continue the conversation with Kennedy because she knew Kennedy was right. Although Kennedy always had on something descent, Cherae never would have felt threatened if she wore something sexy because Cherae didn't find Kennedy sexy, well at least not as sexy as she.

"And like I said, that is bullshit."

"Look Kennedy, I hear you okay? I just happen to like being comfortable and if I hadda known that Julian was still here, I'da put on my robe. Now are we done?" Cherae asked, yelling in Kennedy's face.

"No, we are not done and who the hell do you think you are

yelling at Cherae?" Kennedy said, moving close to her. She didn't appreciate her yelling when she wasn't yelling at her.

"You Kennedy, you always, always have to have something to be in my ear about and I'm so tired of you acting like you are all that and like you are so perfect. Now that you finally got a man to actually stay with your ass for more than a year, you think you doing something. You always talking about my house this and my man this and I am so sick of you being in my ear for every little thing. Back when you were just fucking Travis and he wasn't yo' man, it didn't matter how I walked around here, but now Julian is here, you are in my ear every five minutes," Cher said, getting louder.

Kennedy was astounded by her going off like that and what did Travis have to do with anything? The only reason why she never fussed when she was kicking it with Travis was because he never stayed long enough to witness Cher and her exotic nighties.

"Cherae Monique, you are outta your mind. I don't think I'm all that because I have a man. I've been preaching the same sermon to you before I met Julian. I've been telling your ass to cover up since you we were fifteen and Travis has nothing to do with this conversation, so what is your main fucking problem?" Kennedy asked. They were in each other's face. All Kennedy wanted to talk to her about was coming into the kitchen in that little bitty ass nightgown and now they were about ready to fist fight.

"You," Cherae said, finally being honest. Her anger was mostly because she was jealous.

"Me, I'm your problem Cherae?" Kennedy asked, now confused.

"Yes, you act like you're my damn momma. You're always in my ear with something that I'm doing or not doing. You want me to do things exactly like you want them done."

"Cher, when you live in someone else's home, you have to respect their rules," she said, trying to lower her voice.

"Rules, Kennedy? I'm fucking thirty-four years old and you are in my face with some rules bullshit? I'm your roommate, not your child."

"Cher you are not my roommate, you are a best friend

staying with me. You haven't paid a fucking dime in rent since you've lived here and every utility in this house I pay, Ms. Grown Ass," Kennedy said, giving her grown ass a dose of reality.

Cherae was really angry. The truth did hurt and now she wished she would have just put on her robe before she came in the kitchen.

"Now wait Kennedy. You are the one who said I didn't have to give you anything for rent when I first moved in and you've never asked me to pay a utility."

"Yeah Cherae that was when you first moved in three years ago, when I knew you didn't have it to give. I wanted you to get your shit together and get on your feet and even after you got the job at Ameritech, you still haven't given me anything Cherae and I shouldn't have to ask you. You are grown and you know that water, lights, phone, gas and cable cost money. You know that shit ain't free and I have never asked you to do anything for three years. And you can't simply cover up your ass by putting on some clothes. Why is that so hard Cherae Monique?" she asked. She didn't want to keep going back and forward with Cher. She didn't want things to get that far out of hand, but it did.

"And again Kennedy, I didn't think he was still here. Now, if you'd excuse me," Cherae said and walked away. She went into her bedroom and was relieved to see that Cortez was still sleeping and he didn't hear her business with Kennedy. She opened her drawer, pulled out some sweats and put on a long sleeved undershirt. She was mad as hell and wanted to tell Kennedy to kiss her ass, but she knew she had no place to go. She sat on the bed and took a deep breath to try and calm down. She mumbled under her breath and Cortez turned over.

"Cherae baby, are you okay?" he asked.

"No, no, I'm not okay and I don't wanna talk right now," she said and the tears burned her eyes. She knew Kennedy was right about everything she said and she didn't ask for much from Cherae. She knew Julian was still there, but she was thinking of herself and she wanted him to see her in her little nightgown.

"Are you sure babe?" he asked, rubbing her back, comforting her.

"Yeah, I'm sure," she said and sobbed for a moment. He

didn't push, he just let her cry.

Chapter Seventeen

"Baby relax, don't let her get you so upset," Julian said while massaging Kennedy's shoulders.

"Jay please, I don't want to talk about it," she said, wiggling her body away from him, letting him know to stop massaging her shoulders.

"Okay then, we don't have to discuss it. I just don't want you to let this ruin the rest of our day."

"Why Jay, tell me why does she do shit and then try to turn it on me like I'm the one that's being the bitch," she said, now talking about it and slamming things on the counter.

"Listen baby…, stop…, stop," he said, turning her around to face him. "Come on baby…, come over here," he said, pulling her gently. "Here sit down, let me finish making the food. You just sit for a moment."

"All I've ever done is tried to help her. I just try to help her," she said crying.

"I know babe, but maybe you should stop helping and let her do some things for herself," he suggested. He just hated to see Kennedy upset and didn't want her crying, not about Cher's trifling ass.

"Cherae is like my sister. I am her only family, Jay. I don't know how to not be there for her. I just want her to be considerate of someone other than herself, that's all."

"I know baby, but you've known Cher for a long time and, baby, some people are not changeable. They are who they are," he said, then grabbed the juice from the island and went to pour some more in the glass for her.

"Julian I know, but this is Cherae and I love her. She is not a bad person, she is just self absorbed and she has always been like that. She is used to everyone doing for her and men just give to her and give to her. I don't think she knows how to give back," Kennedy said. Julian handed her the glass of juice.

"Well I say it is time to stop giving her so much. That's why she can't take no for an answer," he said, understanding why Cherae felt like she was going to make him give in to her, because everyone usually did. "You have to make her carry some of her own weight and let her see that she can't have everything she wants. She needs to know she can't just have her way," he said, giving Kennedy advice and thinking of his situation with Cherae as well. Hell, she was so adamant with her pursuit to get him.

"I guess you're right. Maybe if I would stop giving her so much she'd understand that she has to give, too. I'm just as guilty as everyone else. Cher just has needed me since we were kids. Her momma didn't have a lot and she was on drugs. Cherae spent a lot of time with us at my house and my momma started to take care of her too, just like she was hers. And Cher just has depended on me and my family for so long; I guess I'm just accustomed to doing for her.

"Well she's an adult, baby. Start treating her ass like one. Let her pick up half around here."

"Come on now Jay, Cher doesn't make that much and I just can't do that to her. I just have to take it step by step," she said, getting up to finish cooking. By the time Kennedy was done cooking, Cherae and Cortez had come into the kitchen.

"Hey good afternoon, it smells good up in here," Cortez said.

"Hey Cortez, I didn't know you were here. Sit down and join us. There's plenty," Kennedy offered.

"Cortez was just leaving," Cher said, interrupting.

"Yes I was, but I can stay for some good food," he said, taking a seat. Cher stood there with her arms folded.

"Come on, Cherae Monique, sit down and I'll get you two some plates," Kennedy said, trying to make peace.

"I'm not hungry," Cherae said, still upset.

"Come on, Cher..., sit down with us. I made blueberry waffles and I know you love my blueberry waffles; now sit," Kennedy said as she put the hearty dishes of food on the table. Cher, wanting to stay mad, slid into the chair because the food smelled divine and Kennedy was right, Cher loved her blueberry waffles. They ate and mostly Cortez and Julian talked.

"So Kennedy, when am I going to get a chance to hear you sing?" Cortez asked out of the blue. "Word down at Jay's is that you can blow. They say you tear the house down on Karaoke night."

"Oh yeah?" she asked, pouring a little more syrup on her waffle. "I didn't know the word was out."

"Yeah, that's what I heard," he said.

"Cher, why are you telling Cortez about my singing? You know I don't like just singing for people."

"I didn't," she said dryly. She could care less about Kennedy's singing. She thought she was over rated.

"Naw, it was Tony'em at the club talking about it."

"Oh, Tony was the one running his mouth?" she asked jokingly.

"Yep," he said and Julian smiled

"Yes, this woman got some chords on her. It's a shame she ain't doing it for a living."

"Well my love, some of us don't like the spotlight. We all don't want to be the center of attraction," she joked.

Cher knew that comment was about her. "What does that supposed to mean?" Cher asked, getting serious.

"Oh boy, here we go," Kennedy said and wished she hadn't made that last statement. "Nothing Cherae, it meant nothing," she said, trying to avoid another argument.

"You meant something Kennedy," Cherae barked.

"No I didn't Cher and please, don't make it into something," she begged.

"You know what? You get on my *muthafuckin'* nerves Kennedy," she said and Kennedy dropped her fork. Cortez and Julian looked at Cherae like she had transformed into another person.

"What?" Kennedy asked, surprised to hear Cherae speaking

that way to her.

"You heard me," she said, standing. "You think you are better than me huh Kay?" she yelled, moving toward Kennedy like she wanted to box.

"Cherae, calm your ass down and stop being a drama queen okay," Kennedy said, starting to clear the table. She was so not in the mood to deal with Cher.

"Cher baby, come on..., sit down," Cortez said.

"No, I wanna know what she meant by her little comment."

"Cher, I'm not for this right now, so please gon' on and drop it okay," she said and proceeded to clear the table. "Baby, do you need anything else?" she asked Julian.

"Naw baby, let me help you," Julian said, getting up.

Cher still stood there, waiting on Kennedy to answer her. "Kennedy Renee," she said.

"What Cher, what," Kennedy said, putting the plate down. She turned her attention to Cher. "Why can't you just drop it? You're making something outta nothing."

"No I'm not; I just want to know what you meant. Are you implying that I like being the center of attention? That I like the spotlight?" she asked.

Kennedy was ready to just tell her ass the truth so that they could be done with the bullshit.

"Yes Cherae Monique, that's exactly what I meant. You are an attention seeker, a spotlight hog and you love for all eyes to be on you. And when they are not, you are jealous and you act like no one deserves more than you. Now, are you satisfied?" Kennedy said and went back to clearing the table.

"No, I'm not satisfied and yes I like to be the center of attention. I can't help that I normally get all of the attention where ever I go. It's been that way all of my life."

"Whoop-tee-do Cherae, you're beautiful, the entire city of Chicago knows you're beautiful. Now what? You are even beautiful right now, covered up for a change. But, you have to realize that there are others around you and we too have qualities that people take notice to, so stop trippin' out when someone else is getting the glory," she said.

Cher got even angrier because in her mind, as crazy as it

was, she was the one who was supposed to have it all and Kennedy's fat ass was not supposed to be happier than she, because she was the beautiful one that deserved it all.

Kennedy was simply trying to make a little point and now they were barking at each other again. Cher got more heated because whenever they argued; because Kennedy would always be right and made her feel stupid by the time they were done, just like she was feeling now. So, with nothing else to argue or say, she brought up the clothes thing again.

"See Kennedy, you see how you are?"

"What now Cherae, what did I say this time?" Kennedy asked, exhausted and so was Julian. Cortez sat there wondering why he cared about Cher so much, because she wasn't too bright.

"The clothes thing, you made mention of what I wear again," she said, sounding like a retard.

"What..., what?" Kennedy asked, looking at her confused and shaking her head.

"You are still mad about the nightgown, aren't you? That's why you made that comment," Cher asked, still seeking to keep up hell. She was so angry and just wanted to make Kennedy feel some of her pain.

"Baby, I'm going upstairs," Julian said, not being able to take it anymore. Cherae was hopeless he thought as he kissed Kennedy on the cheek.

"You know what Cherae, I'm going to head out," Cortez said, standing to leave. They didn't want to continue to witness Cher's fanatical behavior and that made her more infuriated. Finally, she said what Julian prayed she'd never say and what Kennedy would have never thought in a million years she'd hear.

"Okay, Ms. Kennedy..., Ms. My Life Is So Great. Cher is the one that is out there and has issues, yea I'm the fucked up one. Since I'm so fucked up, why has your man been trying to fuck me? He must think I'm the center of attraction and the show stopper since he's been trying to get me in bed," she said, acting like she had just announced the cure for cancer.

Cortez stopped, Julian froze and Kennedy almost dropped the dish she had in her hand.

"What..., what did you say, Cherae?" Kennedy asked,

turning to her. Julian turned to come back to the kitchen with his eyes bulging.

"Cherae, don't even fucking lie like that. What the fuck is wrong with you?" Julian asked.

"Cherae, I know I didn't hear what…, I think…, I…," Kennedy was trying to ask, but couldn't quite finish her question.

"Yep, yo' man Julian, been trying to hit it since y'all been together and tried to creep in my bed several nights before going up to yours after he came in from the club," she said, lying like it was nothing.

"Cherae, why are you doing this?" Julian asked, looking at her. He knew that this whole scene was bad.

"Julian, what is she talking about?" Kennedy asked him and he turned to her.

"Baby, do not listen to her, she is lying through her teeth."

"Julian, how you gon' stand there and lie like that? You know you've been trying to get at me for the longest. Just last night you tried to undress me in your fucking office," she said, feeling proud of herself. Now she had the upper hand.

"Undress you…, Cher you are the one who came into my office and took yo' damn clothes off," he said, trembling. "Baby, I swear this bitch is lying," he said. "Cherae tell her the fucking truth, why are you fucking lying. What's wrong with you?" he yelled, moving toward her. Cortez stepped up like he was going to protect her and Julian stopped in his tracks. He wasn't worried about Cortez, but he wasn't about to fight in Kennedy's house either. "Baby, you know what? I'ma tell you the truth, she is the one who has been trying to fuck. Now what?" he said, but it didn't matter. Kennedy was crying already. "Baby listen," Julian said, trying to comfort her.

"Take your hands off of me," she said, snatching away. "Cherae I'm going to ask you this one time. Are you telling me the truth? I mean Cherae, are you telling me the honest to God truth?" Kennedy asked, looking at her.

"Why would I lie about something like this? I have no reason to stand here and lie," she said with a straight face and Kennedy's mind was blown.

"Then why are you telling me now?" Kennedy yelled.

"Because she is lying baby. I don't want Cher. Why would I do that? It's her baby and it's been her from the very beginning and now she gon' stand here and come out of her mouth and say it was me. Baby, I would never," he said, confusing Kennedy.

She turned to him. "Well Julian, if you say it's her, then why didn't you tell me, huh?" she yelled. He and Cherae started going back and forth yelling and accusing each other. "Shut up, just shut up, the both of you. Just shut the hell up," she yelled, making them stop. "Julian please tell me the truth, baby" she pleaded. She wanted him to confess or Cherae to confess. She wanted for them to tell her the truth. She didn't want to believe it was either of them, but she had to know who the guilty one was.

"Baby, I swear…," Julian tried to say.

"You liar," Cher yelled, interrupting him. "Kennedy you know I wouldn't make something like this up," Cher said.

"Then why wait 'til now to tell me something like this Cher? Why would you not tell me?"

"Because…," Julian tried to say.

"Shut up Jay, I'm talking to Cher."

"Kay, I… I," Cher said, stuttering. She was lying and Kennedy didn't know who to believe.

"Julian please get your shit and leave," Kennedy told him.

"Aw, babe…, you gon' stand here and listen to her?" Julian asked, moving in front of Kennedy. "Don't do this. This bitch is evil and she is crazy and I swear she is lying," Julian said.

"Don't touch me," Kennedy told him as he tried to reach for her. She put her hands over her face and her muffled cries made it obvious that it would be useless right now to talk, so he turned to leave the kitchen. Cherae smiled as he walked by, but removed her smile after Kennedy looked up from her hands. Cortez had his eyes on Kennedy, hoping she'd be okay, so he didn't see the little smirk Cherae gave Julian when he walked by.

"Kay, I'm so sorry," Cher said, trying to embrace her.

"You get out too," Kennedy said and Cher almost passed out.

"Kennedy you don't mean that," she asked nervously. That was not how she wanted things to turn out.

"Yes I do, now get your shit and get outta my damn house."

"Kay you can't put me out. Where am I supposed to go?" she whined.

"You are a grown ass woman, so figure it out," she said and walked out of the kitchen. She was headed for her office, which was one of her other spare rooms on the main level, but Cherae was on her heels.

"Kay please don't," she begged and Kennedy turned around and scarred her because it looked like she was about to knock her out.

"Cher I said get out, now go!" she yelled and Cherae stood there as Kennedy went into her office and slammed the door. Cortez helped Cherae gather a few things and Julian dressed slowly upstairs and couldn't believe what had just happened. Cher tapped on the door and Kennedy didn't respond, so she and Cortez left. When she heard them leave, she came out and went into the kitchen and then Julian came down to leave.

"Kennedy baby please," he said, but she didn't want to hear him nor did she allow him to speak. He walked toward her because he wanted to wrap his arms around her, but she stopped him in his tracks.

"Goodbye, Julian," she said.

"Just like that?' he asked, pissed off. She didn't give him a chance.

"Julian I don't want to have to call the cops, now go," she said with her back to him. She loved him so much and she couldn't watch him leave. She stood in one spot 'til she heard his car pull out of her driveway. She went to the door to lock it and fell to the floor and cried.

Chapter Eighteen

Kennedy laid in her bed staring at the ceiling. Her face was drenched and her hair was even wet from all of the tears she had shed. She was in her tri-leveled home alone and heartbroken. She had ignored the ten thousand back to back calls from Julian and Cher. Kennedy was the type of person who never beat around the bush and she always tried to tell people the truth and to have two people in her life that she loved to lie to her just upset her even more. She was truly and honestly confused and didn't know what to believe.

She felt like Julian was the one lying because she had known Cher for too long to think that she'd actually go behind her back and try to sleep with her man. If she did, Julian must have wanted to since he never said anything. Then, on the other hand, Julian was a man that she trusted and he could have been with any woman, so why Cher? He had never given her a reason not to trust him and she never could imagine him cheating on her. Not with Cher anyway. Out of all the women he could have messed around with, for him to pick her best friend wasn't settling right with her.

The thing she was confused about was why they would not say anything. If it was Cher, Julian should have told her a long time ago and if it was Julian, why did Cher not tell her from the start. That was why she was so uncertain and didn't know who to trust or believe. She thought back to the evening when Cher told her to *watch him* and she said *don't say I didn't warn you.* She wondered was that her way of giving Kennedy the heads up? She wondered why Cher didn't just tell her the truth before she fell in love with him.

So many questions and what ifs ran through Kennedy's mind. She was angry, hurt and confused and she had no idea of what she was going to do. To think her man wanted her best friend or her best friend wanted her man made her stomach turn. She didn't want to believe it was true on either hand. She wanted to keep Cher in her life because she loved her like a sister. Julian was the first man she had ever loved and she definitely didn't want to be without him. The more she thought about it, the more she got upset. The more she tried to figure it out, the more confused she was. So, she decided not to think about it anymore, or at least try not to.

She got up and went to the bathroom to get some Excedrin because all the crying made her head ache. When she saw her reflection in the mirror, she didn't like what she saw. She looked at herself, seeing a big fat fool, not the sexy, confident Kennedy Renee Banks she thought she was. She was the fat, stupid Kennedy who had been played by her best friend and man. She knew one day she'd eventually get over Julian, but her lifelong friendship was going to be harder to get over. She began to sob again.

Cher was supposed to be the one to stand up for their friendship and help her to not be hurt, but instead, she stood under her roof in her kitchen and was like, *"Now, bitch, I told you that your fat ass ain't gon' be happy,"* like she took pleasure in hurting her. And Julian, how did he utter the words, *"Baby, I love you,"* but didn't protect her from getting hurt by a bitch he knew was stabbing her in the back? She was so hurt and angry. She was disgusted with the both of them. Hell, if Cher wanted Julian that bad, she should have just opened her mouth before Kennedy went out with him.

Kennedy would have rather dealt with that then than now, because she was already in love with him. She would have liked to know the truth before she had fallen for him, but instead, her best girlfriend basically gave her the finger and tried to get him behind her back, according to Julian. She walked around half naked with her sexy ass body in front of her man deliberately and was trying to get his attention from the jump. Kennedy prayed silently that that wasn't the truth about her friend.

She thought about Cher saying he tried to crawl into her bed, right before coming up to her and how he tried to undress her in his office and then he said that she was the one who undressed in front of him and she was even more confused and didn't know who was telling the truth. She sat on her bathroom floor and the cold tile underneath her ass didn't bother her because the pain in her heart overrode her nerve senses. She cried and didn't try to hold in the sounds of her weeping heart. She was loud and the sound in the bathroom was in acoustics.

She heard her phone again. *Your Everything To Me* by Monica let her know it was Julian and she didn't move to get it. She knew she was going to have to change his ring tone immediately because that song was true, Julian had been her everything for the past year. She loved Julian and loved the way he made her body feel. She loved the way he treated her. He made her feel special and things were so perfect when they were together. Finally, the phone stop ringing and she got up and went to her get it. Before she could pick it up, it began to ring again.

"Stop calling me!" she yelled at the phone because it was Julian again. "I don't want to talk to ya lying ass. Call that bitch, Cherae, for comfort. You think you can just go behind my back and try and fuck my best friend and everything between you and I will be okay? Please, you got me mixed up," she shouted and let out a deep breath when the phone stopped ringing. Then, he called again, but she opened the phone and hit ignore so she wouldn't have to hear his ring tone over again. She went into her menu options and deleted his number from her phone.

Before she could put her phone back on the nightstand, he made a fourth attempt to call her and she hit ignore again. That went on for about ten minutes and then she heard the doorbell ring. She stood still for a moment and it rang again, so she went downstairs to answer it. She looked through the peephole and said, *"You got to be kidding me,"* when she saw Julian. "I know damn well you don't expect for me to let you in," she told him through the door.

"Kennedy baby, come on open the door. We need to talk," he said calmly.

"What? Open the door?" she asked him with attitude. "Are

106

you high?"

"What, what are you talking about, Kennedy? Come on now; let me in so we can talk."

"Talk about what? How you want to fuck my friend, Julian? How you told me you love me, but couldn't help wanting to fuck Cherae?" she shouted through the door.

"Kennedy baby, you know that is bullshit and you know I love you. I would never do that. Open the door, babe, so we can sit and talk," he said, wondering why Kennedy was being so difficult.

"Julian who do you think you are? Do you think I'm stupid?"

"No baby, come on open the door."

"No..., go away. Cherae isn't here. You can fuck her now if you want. You don't have to worry about me being in your way."

"Kay why are you acting like this? You know I love you. You know I only have eyes for you. There are tons of women out there Kay and you think I would stoop so low and try to fuck with your best friend?" he asked and Kennedy was quiet. It sounded true, but why would Cher lie on him? "Kay baby, are you still there?" he asked, touching the door softly. She stood there, her eyes welled and she didn't say a word. "Kennedy open the door, babe. We can work this out. Just open the door, please?" he begged and she resisted him.

"Go away Julian and don't come back okay. If you don't leave, I'm going to call the police," she threatened and he was shocked.

"Call the police?" he said. "Kay, come on, you know I didn't come here to hurt you. Why are you talking crazy? I just want to look at you babe. I need you to look at me," he said, leaning closer to the door. He wanted to reach through the wood and hold her tight. "Come on babe, open the door so we can talk and fix this. I love you and I need you so much," he said.

She couldn't take it anymore. "No, no, no, Julian. I want you to go okay. I thought you would never hurt me, but you did and I have nothing more to say to you, so please, leave and stop calling me, okay. Just leave me alone!" she yelled. *'No mercy..., no mercy,'* she whispered to herself. "My daddy warned me about men like you and I fell in love anyway and I see what he meant. You had no mercy on my heart Julian and I want you to leave me alone," she cried.

He knew he wasn't going to convince her, not that night anyway. "I love you, Kennedy. I really do and I wish you could see that I am not the one who is lying. Cher is an evil, jealous bitch and she is not your friend Kay," he said, trying to get her to see Cherae was living foul.

"Oh, now you blame it on Cher? If it's not fucking true Julian, why didn't you tell me? You love me so much, but you couldn't tell me that bullshit before now? You are a liar Julian, so please go," she begged, because the more he spoke, the more she wanted to open the door.

"I didn't try to sleep with that woman Kennedy!" he yelled. He was so angry he wanted to kick in the door. "You got to know I never tried anything with Cherae. I wanted to tell you baby, I did, but I just didn't know how and I thought she'd lay off. Please Kay, I love you," he told her, jiggling the door handle trying to open the door. He was tempted to use his key, but he knew that would not be the right time to come in with her feeling the way she felt.

"I don't care Julian, okay? It's over between us and if you love me you'd leave me alone."

"That's just it Kay, I love you so much that I can't just leave you alone. I am going through hell right now because you mean so much to me and I can't stand the thought of losing you. I can't accept that Kay. I just want to talk to you face to face baby. I need you Kay. My life is so different and so much better now and I don't want to go back to the life I had before I met you. You are the first woman that I've loved like this," he cried.

She shook her head at his words. His words penetrated her heart, but the thoughts of what Cherae said overruled what her heart was feeling and she knew she had to end the conversation.

"No Julian, this conversation is over," she said and moved quickly to get away from her front door. He began to ring her bell and call out her name and she could hear him 'til she got up the stairs to her room. She shut the door, turned on the music and turned the volume up loud. She sat on the ottoman and put her face in her hands and cried.

After a few moments of banging and ringing her doorbell to get her to come back to the door, Julian finally got into his car and left. He pulled out his phone and began calling her again and she powered her phone off. He then called the house and she took the phone off the hook. She calmed herself, turned off the music and went downstairs to clean the kitchen. She wanted to throw the dishes that Cher and Julian used in the trash when she thought of them. As she raked the uneaten food into the trash and she started to cry all over again.

By the time she was done cleaning and crying she was exhausted. She climbed the stairs and took a shower. She crawled into bed and pulled the covers over her head. It was only nine and she wasn't sleepy, but had nowhere to go or nothing to do. She had no man, so going to the club was out and Cherae was gone, so she was alone in her tri-leveled home. For the first time, she felt lonely. She blocked out the thoughts of being at the club with Julian, because that's where she would have been if they were still together.

She tried to not think about how good it would have been to be out with her friends and her man like they usually did on Saturday nights. She tried not to even let her mind go to the good loving Julian usually put on her after he had a few Crown and Cokes in his system. She turned over, asked God for strength and cried herself to sleep.

Chapter Nineteen

It had been four days and Kennedy managed to avoid Julian and Cherae. She took a couple days off and Teresa was glad to be there for her. She had managed to get up and not cry in the shower, so she decided to go to work. She pulled her hair up and went back to her press powder and lip gloss look that she always wore prior to falling in love with Julian. She put on one of her dull navy blue and gray work outfits and headed for the door. She had changed up her work wardrobe after meeting Julian because he often picked her up to take her lunch in the afternoons or dinner after work.

When she walked into her store, her staff could see the change and knew something was different, but they didn't know that she and Julian broke up because Teresa didn't run her mouth or tell other folks business. Kennedy knew she wouldn't. She knew that Teresa was not like her back stabbing, bitch ass, supposed to be, fake ass friend Cherae. She didn't say a word about why Kennedy was not there or when she was coming back. To avoid the weird stares, she went straight back to her office. She sat down and convinced herself that she was going to be okay and she wasn't going to cry. Her daddy and uncles told her a long time ago that men had no mercy on your heart, but she wished they had warned her about best friends too.

She looked at her reflection in the monitor before it came on and that reflection was a stranger. She shook it off and tried to get her books done and make sure her shipment was on its way. She checked her email and put a check mark in every last one that was from Julian and deleted them all. She kept zoning out and couldn't concentrate, so she stood to stretch and take a little break and her cell phone rang. She looked at the ID and it was Cherae, so she put it back on her desk. She didn't want to cry about her situation again, so she blinked back the tears and tried to get back to work. Cher tried calling her again and she hit ignore. After a few minutes of her trying to call, Cher walked into her office and Kennedy was shocked to see her.

"We need to talk," Cher said and shut the door.

"Cher what in the hell are you doing here?" Kennedy asked, taking her glasses off. Cher knew that was a risky move to go to her office, but she thought she had a better chance of not getting her ass whipped at the store verses going to the house.

"I need to talk to you Kay. You won't take my calls and I need to talk to you please," she begged.

Kennedy had nothing to say to her. "Cher, I'm busy and this is not the time or place for this," she said, looking at her like how dare you walk into my place of business to talk about our personal issues.

"Listen Kay please. I need to come home. I have no place to go and I can't keep crashing at Cortez's place. You know I don't have money like that so please Kay, can I come home?" she begged.

Kennedy couldn't believe her ears. "Oh, so you are here to talk about your living situation? No *'hey, Kennedy, I'm sorry for went down last Saturday morning when I announced your man has been trying to fuck me your entire relationship.'* No *'I'm sorry for hurting you, but I need to come home Kennedy, because you know I can't stay at Cortez's,'*" she snapped. She wondered how Cher was so clueless and selfish and only thought about her.

"Kay you know I'm sorry for that. I am sorry for not telling you sooner, but I thought I had Julian under control and you were happy and I didn't want to just tell you that your man is a dog," she said coldly. Kennedy just looked at her. "Kay come on I'm sorry okay, but I need to come home. I am broke please, I'm sorry," she said pathetically. Kennedy felt sorry for her again. She loved Cher and she had a difficult time telling Cher no. "Please, Kay, I'm sorry. I know I should have told you and I am so sorry," Cher said, managing to muster up some fake tears.

"I accept your apology, now get out of my office,"

Kennedy said, trying to stick to her guns. She was still mad and she wasn't ready to let her come home.

"That's it? You just gon' throw me on the streets Kay? You gon' throw away our friendship of forever out the window over Julian's ass? We have been best friends since we were seven and over a man you gon' just do me like this? That is why I didn't want to tell you. I knew you would take his side," she yelled.

"Cher lower your damn voice. This is my place of business," Kennedy said, getting up. "You don't get it Cher. Will you stop thinking about Cherae Monique Thompson for just five minutes? I love Julian. I fell in love with that man and to learn that it was a lie and the entire time you watched me fall deeper and deeper for a man that you knew was dogging me. That turns my stomach to know the man I shared my mind, body and heart with wanted to fuck my best friend," she said.

Cher had a look on her face like she didn't understand and Kennedy wondered if she was getting anything into that empty head of hers. "So, stop for once and think about me Cher," Kennedy said, pointing at herself. "I am miserable, but do you care? You've been gone a few days and every single message you left on my voicemail was about how you don't have money and how you need me and you need to come home. Can I, can I, can I please, are the only words out of your mouth Cher. Not once did you say, *'Kennedy my friend, how are you holding up?'* or *'I hope you're okay.'* And now you come up in here with your weak ass apology and I'm supposed to say okay?" Kennedy said, fighting the tears.

"Kay we are friends and Julian is just a man. Why are you throwing our friendship out the window over him?" she asked.

Kennedy wanted to slap her. "Because I love him Cherae. Did you not hear a word I just said? I lost my man and my best friend in the same damn day and I am fucked up behind that," she barked. Cherae was dumb as a box of rocks, but that was why Kennedy always went out on a limb for her.

"Kay you didn't lose me. I'm right here and I'm begging you to forgive me," she said, trying to reach for Kennedy's hand.

"Cher please just go, okay? Get out of my office. I'm not ready for you to come home right now, so just go," she said, walking back behind her desk.

"Go where Kay? I have nowhere to go. I need to come home. I need my clothes. All of my stuff is at home and I am living at Cortez's with my toothbrush and a couple sets of change of clothes," she said.

Kennedy knew she at least had to allow her to get some more things from the house. "Well you are welcome to come and get anything you need when I get home. I am not trying to keep your things," she said and sat down.

"Kay you are seriously going to believe him over me?"

"Cher I don't know who or what to believe okay? You didn't tell me when you should have told me and neither did he, so you know what? I'm not sure if it was you or him. Now you have the truth that is why I'm not ready to talk to you or let you come home. That is why I am here in my office messed up Cherae Monique. Now, until I feel like I want to get back to our friendship, I don't want to talk to you," she said.

Cherae was floored because she didn't expect to get that reaction from Kennedy. "Okay fine. I will be at Cortez's. When you get home, please call me so I can get some things from the house. If you don't believe me, what can I do? But, let me say this, Julian ain't shit. He is no different from any man out there. If you forgive that motherfucker and go back to him you are going to wish you hadda listen to me. Men are men Kay and we have been friends too long for me to lie," she said and stormed out.

She sounded convincing, Kennedy thought. She did tell Kennedy once before to watch him and Kennedy still keep those words in the back of her head. She wondered if Cherae was telling her truth about Julian.

She tried to get back to work, but as soon as she began to get back on track they buzzed her to come out to the front. She looked at the monitors and saw it was the delivery guy with roses. She got up and went out and looked at Teresa like *'why did you buzz me for this?'*

"I'm sorry Kennedy, but the delivery person said he has special instructions for you to sign," she said.

Kennedy looked at her like *'this man don't know if you are me or not'*, but she saw Teresa's nametag and that was a dead giveaway she was not Kennedy. She scribbled her name and took the roses from the delivery guy. She walked back to the back and put the roses on the round table in the break area. She didn't bother reading the card because she knew they were from Julian.

"Those are beautiful Miss Banks," Tiffany said, coming out of the bathroom.

"You think so?" Kennedy asked.

"Yes ma'am," she said, admiring them. "My cheap boyfriend would never send me roses like these," she joked.

"You can have them," Kennedy told her, walking back to her office.

"Are you serious?" she asked.

"Yep, enjoy them," she said.

Teresa overheard her and snatched the card before Tiffany moved her roses over to the counter.

"Tiffany can you please go out front with Jason while I talk to Kennedy for a moment?" she said and Tiffany did what she asked. She walked into Kennedy's office and she was back to work. Teresa opened the card and sat down in the chair in front of her desk and read it. *"Kennedy my love, I know things turned out very ugly and I have no idea or where to begin to fix it. I love you and I'm missing you so much and I am going insane not being able to talk to you. I didn't do any of the things she said I did and I'm begging you to at least call me. I have to talk to you or else I'm going to go crazy. Love, Julian,"* Teresa said, looking at Kennedy and she didn't look up.

"Thank you," Kennedy said like she didn't hear a word that she read.

Teresa sat there and waited for Kennedy to give an honest reaction, but she was not budging.

"You don't want the card?"

"Nope," she said, looking at the computer screen.

"Are you sure?" Teresa said, waiting on her to stop acting like she didn't care.

"Yes I'm sure and why did you let Cherae in?" she asked, looking at Teresa.

"You know I didn't let Cherae in. She just strolled by me, keyed in the code that you gave her and waltzed back here."

"I know and please when you get a chance change that code," she said, turning back to her computer.

"So, are you going to talk to Julian?"

"Nope," she said.

"Why not Kennedy? You should call him. Give him a chance to tell you what really happened," she said and Kennedy wasn't interested.

"Teresa I told you I never want to see him again," Kennedy said, being a tough girl.

"I know what you said and what you think is going to happen, but I know you love him and I know it is going to be impossible for you to never see him again. What does your heart say, Kennedy?"

"My heart is on mute," she said, stroking the keyboard. Teresa laughed with disbelief. Kennedy wasn't trying to make a joke, so she didn't laugh with her.

"Well do you wanna know what I think?"

"Nope, but I know you are going to tell me anyway," she said, still not stopping what she was doing.

"You're damn right I am," Teresa said, getting up and shutting the office door because she noticed Tiffany back in the break area.

"Go head," Kennedy said, not giving her, her undivided attention.

"Cher is a liar," Teresa said, being bluntly honest.

"How are you going to take his side Teresa? Julian is a man like all men and they all want Cher," she said, giving Teresa her attention.

"Come on Kay listen to yourself. Not every man wants Cher. She is an evil bitch and trust me, the way she wanted Julian that night, I wouldn't put it past her."

"We all wanted Julian that night Teresa, so that doesn't make her a liar. You wanted him too when we saw him," she said, reminding her about the draw.

"Yes okay, that is true, but Cherae was pissed and she even made passes in front of your face. You know Cher can't hold water. As soon as Julian would have hit on her once she would have come running, just to prove that point that she thinks and obviously you too, that every man wants her. Julian didn't chose her that night and I bet any amount of money that she threw herself at him and when he didn't give, that is when she got mad and did what she did," Teresa said, having it all figured out, but no way Kennedy was going to believe that Cher would go that far.

"Ree stop it, okay. I've heard enough. Cher is a lot of things, but she has never tried to mess with any of my boyfriends," Kennedy said, defending her.

"Kennedy Renee you haven't had a lot of boyfriends in your life, especially not one as fine as Julian and we all know how Cher used to flirt with him Kay," she said. Kennedy still didn't want to swallow that.

"I know, but Cher has never done anything so low."

"Yes, except walk around your house half naked in front of him every chance she got, but what do I know?" she said.

"Yes, but Cher is always naked. That was before I met Julian."

"Okay, so then you believe that Julian, the man who has wined and dined you and has spoiled the shit out of you for the past year, not to mention the way you say he stokes your special place like an artist. He has showered you with love and attention and to just go out like that with Cher? Don't make sense," she said.

Kennedy was in a pool of confusion. She didn't want to believe that either of them would do that, but one of them was guilty, but who?

"No Ree, I don't want to believe that Julian would do that, but I've known Cher all my life and Julian for what, a year and some change. He is a man Ree and he is not exempt," she said.

"Okay baby fine, I'm going to get back out here. I love you and I'm sorry that things turned out this way. I just know that you were a different person, a happier person when you were with Julian and I just don't think he is the bad guy, but you know Cherae, that is your friend," she said like she has always said.

"Yes, she is my friend," Kennedy said under her breath when Teresa walked out of her office.

Chapter Twenty

Kennedy finished up at the store and when she was on her way home, she hesitated but called Cherae on her cell phone to tell her she could come by the house for some of her things. She wasn't ready to allow Cherae back to stay, but she knew she didn't take much when she left. When she got home, Cherae was there about ten minutes later as if she was waiting by the phone for Kennedy to call. Kennedy heard her come in but didn't bother to go into her room and speak. She stayed in the kitchen and continued to force her dinner down her throat. She hadn't eaten in a couple of days and she knew she had to eat something before she made herself sick.

After ten minutes of playing with her pasta, she got up and dumped it into the sink and hit the garbage disposal switch. She was about to head upstairs when Cherae came out with a packed bag. She was looking cute of course, and she was covered up for a change with jeans and a sweater. It looked new and Kennedy figured Cortez must have gotten her something to wear 'til she could get some clothes from the house.

"Hey Kay can I talk to you for a second?" she asked. Kennedy paused and she sat on the steps and just waited for her to talk. "Listen, I want you to know that I'm sorry for how I just let it rip on Saturday. You are right, I should have told you from the very beginning about Julian, but I didn't want to cause problems with you and Julian. I mean, you were so happy and I didn't want to ruin that by telling you he was making passes at me. I thought he'd eventually stop and just chill, but when he tried to kiss me and then asked me to take my dress off in his office that night, I said enough was enough. I was prepared to tell you then, it just came out all wrong," she said lying and stood there and waited for Kennedy to respond.

"Cher you had time to tell me. I don't understand why you waited 'til we get into a heated argument and then you just burst out with something like that, like you were deliberately trying to hurt me. And to top it all off, if you knew Julian was living foul, you didn't do much to not encourage him by walking around in front of him half dressed all the damn time. I have witnessed you flirt with him Cher, so I don't see where you were trying to spare my feelings," she said, considering how things looked. They did look bad for Cher more than Julian, but she still wasn't convinced that Cher would do something that evil to her.

"Kennedy I'm so sorry okay," she said, crying. "I know that it looks bad and I picked a horrible way to tell you and I'm sorry, but I'm so glad to have finally gotten it out. I know it came out bad, but I wanted to tell you so many times I swear. It was hard to tell you something like that. I know how you felt about Julian and believe me it was hard. At times I honestly thought you wouldn't have believed me if I hadda told you," she said, wiping her eyes.

"Yes I would have Cher. I have told you our entire lives to always be honest with me, even if it hurts. You are my friend Cher and as my friend it was your responsibility to look after me like I've looked out for you. You were supposed to be my friend, Cher," she said, now crying.

"I know Kennedy please. I'm so sorry. I'm begging you to forgive me. I can't stay at Cortez's too much longer. I don't have money to give him and he is a nice guy, but our relationship ain't on that level for me to be living with him."

"Cher not tonight okay," she said, wanting to just let her stay, but Cher had to know how bad she had hurt her.

"Kay I wanna come home," she cried.

"I know Cher, but you can't tonight."

"Kennedy Renee please, I am sorry and I wouldn't ask you, but I need a few dollars for gas, can you...," she asked with no shame.

Kennedy got up to get her purse. She only had big bills, so

she gave her two hundred dollars.

"Here, this should help you for a few days. Now you have to go Cherae Monique," she said and walked away with tears in her eyes.

Cher didn't argue. She got her bag and left.

Kennedy hadn't heard from Cher for a couple of days and she knew it was because she gave her a little cash. She wasn't even mad about it because she knew Cherae. She knew she would be quiet for a few more days because she gave her money on Wednesday and Cher's payday was that Friday. Kennedy did miss Cher and the house was so empty without her. She was lonely, that was for sure, but she still didn't pick up her phone at any point when Julian called. She was tempted so many times on Friday night because she missed him so much and her body wanted him, but she didn't break.

After he sent her flowers to her house and her job every day, she knew he was thinking of her. That Saturday morning when the deliver guy came with more flowers, she thought about sending them back but she took them anyway. They smelled fabulous, but she still didn't read the card like she hadn't read any of the other cards. She didn't want to hear what he had to say, so she refused to read anything from him. When she checked her voicemail, she hit the seven key to avoid hearing his voice. When he'd text her on her phone, she'd open it and erase it right away, but the words *please, miss you, love and need* would catch her eye.

It had been a week and a day since she got the news in her kitchen and she was doing better. She tried to not think of either of them and not wonder if it was him or her, either way, one of them was wrong and both of them was wrong for not telling her. To have her first love and best friend do her so bad was like a nightmare and putting Julian's stuff in a box was even harder for her that Sunday afternoon.

She had put it off for days and she knew it had to be done because his things were interrupting her healing process. He had drawer space, closet space and the other sink on her vanity housed a few of his toiletry items. After she finished packing his things, she bravely dialed his number to ask him over to get them.

"Hello…, hello, Kennedy, baby, are you there?" Julian said nervously because he dropped the phone when he realized it was Kennedy calling him.

"Yes I'm here Julian. I was just wondering what you wanted to do about your stuff?" she asked. He could not believe she was calling him for that.

"Kay look baby, I don't care about my stuff. I've been going out of my mind and I need to see you Kennedy. Can you just give me five minutes of your time please?" he pleaded.

"Listen Julian, we don't have anything to talk about or discuss," she said coldly. He was so angry with her for treating him so cold and not at least talking to him. After all she claimed she loved him too.

"Babe, how can you say that like we didn't have a relationship Kennedy? I wasn't in a relationship by myself for a year. I was with you," he said and her eyes welled. That was exactly why she avoided him because she was still soft. "Please, Kennedy just talk to me, we can work our thing out, but you got to talk to me. I know you love me and you know I love you woman, so why won't you at least talk to me?" he asked.

"Julian please, okay. I just can't right now. I'm not okay with what happened and I just can't talk to you right now."

"Then when, when you get over me or when you stop crying over me every day? I can assure you that won't happen because we are in love Kennedy and I know if you love me as half as much as you said you did, you are just as miserable as I am. I miss you so fucking much Kennedy and you know I am nuts over you and to cheat on you with your best friend baby? Come on, use your head."

"Oh so I'm stupid now? I'm the one that needs to use my head? Which head were you using when you were trying to fuck my best friend Julian? Or as you say, it was her, right? Which head were you using when you didn't come to me and tell me what was going on? If it wasn't you Julian, you must have wanted a piece of Cher's ass to not tell," she said, getting upset all over again. "Now what in the fuck do you want me to do with your stuff?" she barked.

Julian let the tears roll down his cheeks. What she said made a lot of sense and he understood why she was giving him a hard time and why she was not so easy to just give him a chance.

"Look, I'll come by in about an hour to get my stuff," he said.

"Fine," she said and ended the call.

Julian coming over there wasn't a great idea she thought to herself, but she wanted him to get his things so she could get on with getting over him. She went downstairs and poured herself a drink and then another. She went up and went into the bathroom to pull her hair up. She wished her face didn't look like she had been crying all day, but no matter how many times she put the hot towel on her face, she still looked sad.

When the door bell rang, she didn't look through peephole because she knew it was him. When she opened the door, she was so mad because he was looking so damn good and she wanted to grab him and stick her tongue in his mouth. She wanted to rip away her clothes and let him suck on her nipples and lick her aching body. She had a flash of dropping to her knees and rubbing his dick over lips.

"Hey," he said, snapping her back to reality. All she saw was them naked and fucking in her foyer.

"Hey, your things are right there," she said, pointing to the box. She didn't want that to be a visit, she just wanted him to get his shit and go. He had to because after seeing him, she was weaker than she thought and was tempted to give him some break up pussy.

"I see," he said, acknowledging the box. "You look beautiful," he said and she knew he was lying because she had on an oversized shirt with some pajama pants. Her hair was pulled up in a pony tail and her eyes were swollen from crying. That didn't matter to him though, because he was just happy to see her.

"Yea, whatever," she said and turned away and waited for him to get his box.

"Kennedy baby, please don't do this. I know you are hurt baby, but she came at me," he tried to say.

"Save it," she yelled. "I've heard that shit from you

already. You and Cherae are one of a kind," she said.

He was not happy with that. "Oh no we are not, that hoe has issues," he said.

She cut him off. "Hoe, watch it," she said, giving him the evil eye.

"Look I'm sorry okay, but yo' girl is foul Kennedy. I don't know why she wants to do this to us and I don't know what the fuck is wrong with her, but I put everything I had into this relationship Kennedy and I gave you all of me and as soon as your girl opens her mouth and put some bullshit in your head about me you just put my shit in a box without giving me a chance to explain or even talk to you. I mean, what am I supposed to do Kennedy? Just go about my way like you and I were never together? How can you do that?" he yelled.

"You were not honest with me Julian. I can't understand how you and Cherae can sit around and not consider for a minute how this makes me feel and how this hurts."

"I have thought about that Kennedy and I have tried to talk to you. I have told you nothing happened with me and Cher, but you don't want to hear that."

"I want to hear the truth Julian," she yelled.

"And I'm telling you the truth dammit," he yelled and she was done. His truth, whatever that was, should have come a long time ago.

"No Julian, you were not honest with me from the very beginning, so we are in this predicament because you didn't tell me what was going on. I don't want to believe it was you baby, I don't. You're right I miss you like crazy and I miss what we had, but I don't know what happened or who did what. I close my eyes Julian and I can't see how Cherae would, like I can't see how you would. You and Cherae were the closest people to me and the both of you played me. Now go Julian, get your stuff and please go," she said, crying. He wanted to hold her so bad, but he knew she didn't want him to touch her.

"Kay please baby, don't. I want to stay and hold you," he said and she backed up.

"Don't Julian, I want you to go," she said, wiping her tears.

"I'm sorry," he said and got the box. "I love you baby and

I'm sorry," he said, looking at her with tears in his eyes. It was killing him to see her hurt.

"Yea me too," she said and didn't look at him. He grabbed the box and finally walked out. She hurried and locked the door and slid down to the floor and cried.

Chapter Twenty One

Cherae was home and things were not quite back to normal, but they were okay. She and Kennedy were talking, but things still were a little weird. Julian had finally done what Kennedy asked him to do and stop calling her and stop sending her flowers. She missed him like crazy and wanted to call him many times, but she didn't. After three months, winter had approached and Kennedy felt lonelier as the days went by. Cher was still kicking it with Cortez and Teresa's man was still with her. All was well with Kennedy, but she still cried from time to time. Julian was the first and last man she loved and she could not let go. She found herself daydreaming and fantasizing about him all the time.

She'd drive by the club and see his car and want to go in just to say hi, but she knew that would have not been a good idea. Plus, she figured he was doing fine without her.

"Hey Kay, you got a second?" Cherae said, tapping on her room door.

"Yea what's up?"

"Well Cortez asked me to go away with him this weekend," she said, smiling.

"Wow Cher, that's great. Where is he taking you?" Kennedy asked while she wrapped her hair.

"To this ski resort in Colorado, but here's the thing, my pay period is next week," she said.

Kennedy knew it was money. "Cher, if he is inviting you, why are you worried about money?"

"Because Kay, I can't go out of town broke. What if we get into it or if something happens and I need to get home?" she said, whining like she always did.

"Then make him get you home," she said, walking past her and going down the steps and Cherae followed her.

"Come on Kay. You know I can't go with no money."

"Cher I told you that I was going to stop giving you cash. You never pay me back and...," she tried to say and Cherae started to plead.

"Come on Kay please? I will pay you back this time and if I don't need it I will give it back to you."

"Cherae Monique, do you know how many times you have told me that?"

"Maybe a million, but I just can't go on this trip broke. Please Kay, please."

"You can go broke," she said and poured herself a drink.

"Kennedy Renee," she said, looking at her like *'you can't be serious.'*

"Cherae Monique," she said, looking at her like *'I am dead serious.'*

"Come on Kay, please? I'm begging you. I want to go skiing and I can't go with twenty eight dollars," she said.

"Okay Cher dang, you get on my nerves," she said and Cher jumped and hugged her.

"Oh thank you, thank you, thank you," she said and took a swallow of Kennedy's drink and Kennedy took her glass out of her hand.

"How much and when are you leaving?" she asked, going into the fridge.

"Tomorrow after work and whatever you give me is fine," she said because she wasn't going to be picky, she was happy to just be getting money from Kennedy period.

"Okay, I will go by the cash station tonight, that way I don't have to worry about getting it to you tomorrow."

"Okay and thanks Kennedy," she said sincerely.

"You're welcome," she said with a smile, thinking to herself that things were back to normal.

"Kennedy," he said and she froze. She knew it was him and

she turned around slowly.

"Hi, Julian," she said, surprised to see him.

"How have you been?" he asked.

"Good, I…, um…, I'm…, good," she said, taken off guard by the woman he was with.

"You're looking good," he said as if the gorgeous model chick wasn't standing next to him and holding his arm. She had on a long coat and matching hat and her face was beautiful and Kennedy could tell she was petite.

"Thanks, so are you," she said, feeling awkward.

"Hello," the woman said, speaking to Kennedy.

"Hi," Kennedy returned with a smile.

"I'm Rona, Julian's girlfriend" she said, introducing herself because Julian didn't bother. He was just staring at Kennedy.

"Um, I'm Kennedy," she said, being polite wanting to say *'Julian's ex girlfriend,'* but she didn't and Julian's eyes were locked on her.

"Jay, we should be going babe," she said, snapping him out of his daydream.

"Oh yes, um Kennedy, it was so good to see you," he said, looking at her like he wanted to say more.

"You too," she said and hurried out of the grocery store doors. She rushed to her truck, sat there and tried to get herself together. The tears burned and she clenched the steering wheel. How on earth could she run into him at the local grocery store? Him being with another woman didn't make her feel good at all.

She knew he wasn't thinking of her fat ass anymore for sure with one of the Bratz dolls on his arm. She was looking like shit with no make up and a stupid ponytail in her hair with her big bubble winter jacket, not a cute trench like the model he had on his arm that was holding on to him like Kennedy was going to put him in her purse.

Kennedy let the tears flow and wished she had her man back. She was lonely and Cher was going on skiing trips. If it wasn't for Cherae, she wouldn't have went to the stupid store anyway. "Damn!" she yelled before cranking the ignition. She looked out of her rearview mirror and saw them walking to Julian's car. It looked like they were arguing from the way Rona was twisting her neck and pointing her finger. Julian unlocked the door and opened it for her, but all the neck twisting Rona was doing made him walk off without closing it.

She wiped her tears on her gloves and wondered if they were arguing because he didn't introduce her or because he stared at her a little too long. She wanted to get out and tell Rona she was too beautiful to worry about her, because she knew Julian wouldn't leave her perfect size three to come back to her fat ass. She pulled out of the parking stall and cried all the way home. She missed him and wanted him back. Hell, she let Cher come back and she still didn't know the truth, so why couldn't she go back to him.

When she got home, she overheard Cher on the phone and she figured she'd come upstairs when she was done. Kennedy peeled off her clothes and looked at the clock, wishing she was getting ready to go to the club with Julian instead of being in the house again by herself. She wanted to at least ask him if he missed her like she missed him. She turned on the shower and got in. She showered and thought about how Julian used to make her body scream. She thought about how he used to lick her body, sending her almost into a seizure. She closed her eyes and let the hand held sprayer massage her erect nipples and then she moved it down between her legs.

She fell back against the wall and played back an episode of Julian making love to her in her mind and she cried when her body orgasm because she missed the way he used to treat her. She missed his smile and his presence. She thought about what he said to her on the last day he came over to get his things. The words were programmed into her head.

"Do you just expect for me go about my way like you and I were never together?"

"No Julian, because I can't," she said, answering his question. She turned off the water and got out and put on her robe. She was sitting on her ottoman putting on lotion and Cher tapped.

"Come in," she said.

"I heard you come in a little while ago," she said and noticed she had been crying. "What's wrong with you?" she asked, frowning her face. Kennedy hated when she did that.

"I ran into Julian," she said with her head down.

"Where?" Cher asked with what Kennedy thought sounded like excitement.

"At Jewel's," she said, putting the cap on her lotion.

"Oh, what did he say? Did he say something?"

"Something like what Cherae?"

"I don't know Kay," she said nervously. "Since you were crying I figured he may have said something to upset you."

"He didn't say anything, but he was with a woman," she said, getting up walking over to her dresser.

"What woman?" she asked, frowning her face again.

"I don't know Cher, some young chick."

"Oh, so why are you upset?"

"Well Cher, I'm not over him and seeing him just sparked some memories."

"Oh well anyway, did you get the money?" she asked, not concerned about what she said about the old memories.

Kennedy had never mourned over her relationship with Cherae. Teresa was the only one there for her emotionally after the break up and she wondered why Cherae was so insensitive to her feelings. She acted as if she had no clue that Kennedy and Julian were in love and the break up was an emotional tornado for Kennedy, so Kennedy got her purse, pulled out her wallet and gave her ten twenties. She counted it in front of Kennedy.

"Hey, can I get three?" she asked with no shame.

"No and you lucky you got that Cher," Kennedy snapped.

"Dang Kay, I was just asking," she said.

"And I am just answering. You're going out of town with him and I know he got this trip so...," Kennedy said looking at her like she was ungrateful.

Cher knew she was about to fuss. "Alright, alright, Kay, don't start."

"Start what?" she asked, giving her the same frowning face she gave her.

"Fussing, I get tired of hearing you fuss," she said.

"I get tired of you asking me for money," she said and Cher didn't say anything. "If Julian was taking me out of town, I could leave my money right here and he would treat me to any and everything because that's the kind of man I had, but you don't give a shit about that," Kennedy said, venting.

"What do you mean Kay, I didn't break y'all up."

"Nope you didn't, all you did was not be there for me when we did," she said.

"What are you talking about Kay? You threw me out!" she yelled.

"And I let you come back and you and I are still together, but the only man that I ever loved is gone. Gone and do you even know how much I miss him or how many nights I've been up in here crying my eyes out over him? Julian may have messed up, Cherae, but he loved me."

"Julian did not love you Kennedy," she snapped, with disgust.

"How would you know?" Kennedy asked getting in her face.

"He wanted me, Kennedy."

"Well Cherae if he wanted you, he would have been with you. Newsflash, no matter what you said about Julian. I spent a year and four months with him. He put a smile on my face for that time and if you were so fucking irresistible Cher, I would have watched him spend all his time with you. However you say my man was behind my back is probably right, but you don't know what we shared," she cried.

"What's wrong with you Kennedy? You're defending him after what I told you he did? Are you that desperate?"

"What did you just say?" she asked.

"You heard me. How could you defend him after he tried to damn near rape me?"

"Let me tell you something, Cherae Monique. I'm not desperate and if I was so hard up, he'd be here and your ass would be on the streets. I struggled back and forth on what to do and the only reason why you are here and not him is because I love you like a sister. Sometimes I think I love you more than myself.

"You and my daddy are the closest things to me now and each and every day I pray and hope that you told me the truth and didn't do what Julian accused you of doing. Now, if I say things in Julian's defense it has nothing to do with me being fucking desperate. It's because the man I fell in love with Cher, is not the man you described and I pray to God that I made the right decision because the way you do me sometimes I wish I would have chose him over you," she said, crying. "So, any negative thoughts you got in your head about me baby or whether you think I'm fat, desperate, stupid or whatever the case may be. You stop and look back where you and I have come from and you ask yourself who has made the most sacrifices in this relationship. Me," she said, pointing to herself. "I can't believe you sometimes Cher. Do you ever stop to think about my feelings?" she asked.

Cherae remained quiet. She heard everything Kennedy said and felt horrible for the first time for what she did to her. Kennedy had been there for her emotionally, monetarily and as a friend since they were seven and she messed up her relationship with Julian because of her lust and jealousy. She felt so bad for the first time and she never stopped to think about the damage she had done. She never stopped to think of anyone other than herself. Now she was standing in front of Kennedy wishing she would have never done what she did. The very first time Julian told her that he was in love with her friend she should have respected that and moved on. She never should have made a move on her friend's man in the first place and now she saw that Kennedy was so good to her and she didn't deserve any of what happen.

"I'm sorry Kay. I'm so fucking sorry. I never meant to hurt you and I should have just not said anything. Julian is a good guy and what I said about him...," she was about to say it, but she didn't. She knew if she would have told Kennedy she lied, Kennedy would have never forgiven her. Kennedy was praying that she would say she had lied so she can go back to her man, but she didn't. "He flirted and I just should have ignored it and not said anything and then eventually he may have stopped," she said, sticking to her story.

"No Cher, he wouldn't have stopped. If Julian was trying to get with you, that's not the man I'm meant to be with and I'm hurt now, but eventually I will get over him," she said, believing Cher was really telling the truth. Julian wasn't who she thought he was and she had to just except that.

"Kay, I'm so sorry and I should have given you emotional support. I know it hurts to have your heart broken Kennedy Renee,

I've been there. You were just so mad at me, so I avoided the Julian issue but believe me, I'm sorry for the way things turned out and I'd give anything to make things right," she said, crying too.

"Cherae just try to be there for someone other than you. All the things I do for you are because I love you Cherae Monique and I care about you, not to throw it in your face."

"I know Kay and you have done so much for me and I appreciate everything. I'm gonna get my shit together. No more bullshit. I'm gonna be thirty-five next week and it's time for me to get my life together and stop depending on you for so much. I love you so much Kennedy Renee and you are my only family. Your momma and daddy was there for me and when your momma died, you and your daddy still fed me, took care of me and did things for me that my own momma didn't do. You are my heart and I've been a selfish bitch when all you've done is put up with my shit and help me. I've been a jackass," she said and Kennedy didn't argue. "Listen, I'm sorry. I do care about your happiness," she said and they hugged.

Kennedy was so happy that they had finally had that conversation and hoped Cherae would change. They cried and talked a little while longer and then Cher went downstairs. She threw on some clothes and headed to the club.

Chapter Twenty Two

"Hey Tony, where's Julian?" Cher asked, leaning on the bar.

"He upstairs, what's going on...," he tried to say but she was off.

She ran up the steps. She tapped on the door but walked in before he told her to come in. He was with the woman she assumed Kennedy saw with him earlier. "Oh Jay I'm sorry, but I really need to talk to you. It's about Kennedy," she said.

Julian instantly got nervous. "What is it? Is she hurt? What's wrong, what happened to Kennedy?" he asked in a panic.

"Can we talk in private?" Cherae asked.

"Yes sure. Rona can you please?" he said. She gave him an evil look. That was the shit he hated about dating because Kennedy wasn't like that.

"Hi, I'm Rona, Julian's woman," she said.

Cherae didn't care what or who she was. She was young and pretty and Cher knew her kind because she used to be her ten years ago. "Nice to meet you Rona, now do you mind?" she asked, not shaking her hand. She folded her arms and watched the young beauty stomp out of Julian's office with an attitude. As soon as she shut the door, Julian began drilling her.

"Now what happened? Is Kennedy okay? I just saw her a couple hours ago, is she okay?" he asked, not giving Cherae a chance to explain.

"She's not hurt Julian, so relax okay? However, she is miserable without you Julian. You gotta do something," she said.

"Look Cherae I don't know what you are up to, but it's

because of you that we are no longer together," he said, getting up from his desk.

"I know and I feel horrible, but you have to go to her Jay. Beg, romance her, do whatever because she loves you."

"Cher why don't you tell her the truth? That would help me. I love her more than anything, but she thinks I'm a two timing loser and I can't win her back when she thinks something like that about me."

"Yes you can, you have to send her flowers, poetry, jewelry or something Jay. She is in love with you and I hate what I did," she cried.

"Then tell her the truth. Tell her you lied," he yelled.

"I can't Jay she is my best friend and that would destroy her."

"No Cher that would destroy you. You are the sad reason that she and I are no longer together and you are here in the same office you stripped naked in, begging me to make things happen that I can't without you telling the truth."

"You can Julian, don't you hear me, she still loves you," she said, trying to convince him to make a move.

"But she doesn't trust me Cherae. Use your brain for once. I know you are more than just a pretty face. You can help us by telling her you lied."

"And then I'll lose her," she cried.

"How in the fuck you think I feel? I walk around everyday wanting my woman back. You didn't care that I lost her when you went running off at the mouth and lying and shit."

"Julian stop acting like you are perfect, we had oral sex," she spat.

"No and don't ever say that shit again. You came in and you put my dick in your mouth while I was sleeping in your best friend's bed. I've never flirted or came on to you Cher, so get it out of your head that I did something with you because it was all you. You are the one who deserves to be without Kennedy, not me. You are a narcosis and you can't see it," he yelled. He was mad and angry and he wondered why Cher's alien leaders didn't teach her that shit before they sent her here. She was clueless and all about herself and didn't take responsibility for anything she had done.

"Okay, okay, Julian you are right, it was me, but you still have a chance. I did my best friend wrong and I'm sorry for what I did and I just want her to be happy again. You made her happy, Julian and whatever you gave her she needs in her life again. Please, just call her, beg her. Do whatever, just go back to her."

"If you truly want her to be happy you will tell her the truth," he said.

"I can't," she said, putting her head down.

"Please Cherae, I'm so miserable without her and I need her just as much as she needs me," he pleaded.

"What about baby girl?" she asked, referring to Rona.

"What about her?" he said, not worried about her.

"Look Jay, I'm leaving tomorrow. I will give you my key or whatever, just go over there set things up while she is at work and sweep her off her feet."

"Cher again, I would love to do that. You think I don't want to go to her right now and hold her? She won't even look me in my eyes because of what you put in her head. Now, if you want us to be happy, go home and tell her the truth," he begged.

"Julian, I'm sorry, but I can't do that. I love Kennedy and I can't stand and tell her what I did. I can't hurt her like that. She let me move back home and she forgave me. She would never speak to me again if I told her. I can't," she said, refusing to go home and just do the right thing.

"Cher I lost my woman and my relationship over your lies and bullshit. I have been without the woman I love for four fucking months and you mean to tell me that you can't come clean and just tell her that you were lying? What is so fucking hard? If you want your friend to be happy you will tell her," he said, just hoping she'd get it in her head that the only way there was a chance for him and Kennedy to work it out was if she told the truth. He didn't want to go begging when she still thought of him as a two timing loser.

"Look Jay, are you going to go over or not?"

"I'm not. I don't have a leg to stand on with Kennedy if she still thinks I tried to fuck her best friend Cherae. Why do you not comprehend that?"

"What are you not comprehending Julian? I hear what you

are saying and I know where you are coming from, but I'm not ready to give up my best friend. I feel like shit for what I did to her relationship with you and I want you guys back together Julian, but I'm not going to lose my best friend over this, that's why I can't tell her. All you have to do is go to her and tell her you made a mistake and it was just a little flirting and maybe I took it out of context, but convince her to take you back and she will be happy again."

"So you want me to lie to Kennedy, take the blame for what you started and see if she forgives me and take me back?"

"Yes, that's the plan. She will give you another chance, I know she will."

"No now if you would kindly leave Cherae, I need to get back to work," he said, sitting back at his desk. The idea of him finally getting Kennedy back was great, but no way was he going to admit to the bullshit Cherae was trying to get him to admit to.

"Fine then it's your lost. I hope you're happy," she said.

He didn't even look up at her evil ass. She claimed to love Kennedy so much, but she still didn't want to tell the truth to make it right, so Julian had nothing left to say to her.

Chapter Twenty Three

Kennedy pulled up to her house and was feeling pretty good. She hadn't cried that day and she was feeling happy for a change. She was glad to have a few days alone without Cher being at the house and was anxious about the upcoming weekend. She stopped and had her trucked detailed and stopped by one of her favorite wing joints to get hot wings and beer.

That was something she used to love ordering at the club and she had a taste for it. When she pulled into her driveway, she was beaming and thanked God for how lovely her day had gone because she hadn't had a really good day in months. She wondered if it was because she and Cherae talked the night before and she finally came to terms with her life and what happened with Julian, or if it was because she truly finally believed that Cherae was telling her the truth.

She got out of her truck, walked up the porch and tilted her head wondering who left the note on her door. She snatched it off the door, went inside and went into the kitchen. She put everything on the island expect for the note. She took off her coat, sat on the sofa and opened the envelope. It said Kennedy Banks but did not say who it was from.

When she opened it she knew it was from Julian and although she didn't want to, she read it because she could not resist. By the time she was done, she grabbed her phone and called Teresa to come over to read the letter and console her. She thought that she had closure and was settled with the break up and continuing her lifelong friendship with Cher, but after reading the letter she felt otherwise.

"Kay stop pacing the floor and sit down," Teresa said. Kennedy was trembling and walking back and forth while she was trying to read the letter.

"Ree I can't, okay. Just read the letter," she instructed.

"I can't with your shadow going back and forth. Sit down, please," she said. Kennedy sat and started to clap her knees together.

"Kay," she said grabbing her thigh. "Relax."

"Just read, please."

"Okay," she said and started over. That time, she read it out loud. *"Kennedy, how have you been baby? I've been cool I guess, well, I thought I was cool 'til I saw you last night and you looked amazing. Seeing you made me realize how much I miss you and how much I miss kissing your lips and touching your body, but that is an entire different subject. I'm sure you know how I feel, because I know you have to feel the same, that's if what we had was just as good to you as it was to me. However, the reason for me sitting down to write this letter is because I know if I'd have called, you wouldn't answered and if I'd have come by, no way you would have let me in, so I'm taking my chances on you not ripping this letter to shreds. I saw your so called best friend last night. She came by the club and it's funny because for the first time since I've known that woman, I never knew she had a heart or could care about anyone's needs or feelings but her own, but last night she came here to apologize to me for destroying our relationship and she literally begged me to go to you and fix it. She told me how miserable you were without me and I told her the only way our thing could be fixed is if she told you the truth and even after she stood and cried and said how much she loved you and wanted you to be happy, she could not tell you that she lied. Now, I was stumped. I asked her how can I go back to my woman when my woman thinks that I'm a two timing, low down, dirty dog that tried to fuck her best friend and she told me to just say I flirted and she took it out of content, which made no sense to me and that's when I decided to do what I wanted her to do baby and that's tell you the truth. Since she doesn't love you enough to just simply say, 'Kennedy, I lied,' is beyond me, but I love you so much that I'm going to give you the raw truth and as you said to me before, even if it hurts. So here goes,"* Teresa read and went on to read each and every evil detail of what went down. By the time she finished the six paged letter, Kennedy was shaking.

"So?" Kennedy said, sitting there with tears in her eyes.

"Kennedy you don't want to hear what I have to say," Teresa said, stuffing the letter back into the envelope.

"Yes, yes I do," Kennedy cried.

"I think that bitch did everything he said she did and I think you should kick that bitch out and go back to Julian."

"So, you think Jay is telling the truth?" she asked, trembling. How could she? How could Cher stab her in the back over and over again?

"Kennedy Renee, you don't want me to tell you the obvious baby. How in the hell would he know Cher went out of town if she didn't go by there last night?"

"Well maybe she went by there in attempts to help us get back together and maybe Julian was with his new woman and he and Cher had some words and he...," she said.

Teresa yelled, "Stop, stop it, okay..., stop doing that."

"Doing what?" she asked, confused.

"Making excuses for that bitch. She is a lying bitch and you have to face it. Wake up Kennedy, you are too smart to be stuck on stupid when it comes to Cher," she yelled. Kennedy sobbed.

"No Ree, Cher is my sister. Cher loves me, she is a lot of things, but," she cried. She knew she was avoiding the obvious. She broke down and just faced the facts, Cher was the guilty party. Teresa sat down and held her while she cried. "Ree, we have been through everything together. We lost our teeth in second grade at the same time. Our first of every experience has been shared together, our periods, breast, make-up, clothes. I can't..., I can't..., he is a liar, throw that letter away. Give me that," she said, snatching it and ripping it up. Teresa felt so bad for her.

"Stop Kay, stop," she said, grabbing her and shaking her. "Listen dammit; Cher is not the sister that you are to her. She is a selfish, self serving, narcissistic bitch and she tried to fuck your man. Julian is a good man and that little bitch finally feels sorry for what she did, so fucking what. She has lied time after time and has used you up. I have stood and watched you time after time, year after year, support her, take care of her and be there for her.

"For once, be there for yourself and save yourself. You have to stop walking around making excuses for that grown ass woman. She did it Kennedy, she did this," she said, picking up the half of letter that was on the floor. Kennedy fell to the ground and cried. "I know baby, I know," Teresa said and held her. They sat in the middle of the living room for almost an hour before Kennedy stop sobbing and was able to speak.

"What do I do Ree?" she asked, looking her in the eyes.

"You get up and take care of you. You call your man and talk to him and you start to work on your happiness. You put her ass out and cut it off," she said bluntly.

"I can forgive her if she tells me the truth," she said because she loved Cher so much.

"Yep you can, that is what you are supposed to do. I would never suggest you not forgive her, but forgiving her has nothing to do with you letting her stay under your roof and you continue to support her. You know as well as I do that you are not going to be able to just get back to normal with her."

"I know Ree, I know."

"Do you love Julian?"

"Yes girl, please that is without question," she said, smiling. Something she thought at one point she'd never be able to do when she thought of him.

"Do you believe he loves you?"

"Yeah, I know he does. He is a good man Ree and he treated me like silk."

"Well we have to get him back," she said, helping Kennedy off the floor.

"I know, but that won't be tonight. I'm exhausted and I look like hell," she said, rubbing her hair.

"You do look busted," Teresa said and they laughed.

"Gee, thanks," she said.

"Don't worry, tomorrow he will be there for you," she said. Teresa stayed the night with Kennedy.

The next day, they closed the store early and went shopping. Kennedy got her hair, nails and feet done. She planned to go out that night in hopes to get Julian back. She was still not sure how she was going to handle Cher, but she knew she was going back to her man. Teresa was a good friend and Kennedy was so happy to have her be the straight up and forward person to help her to realize what was right in front of her. Cher was an evil bitch for doing what she did. Kennedy laughed when she thought about the letter when Julian wrote about Cher squeezing behind her chair in her room. She kept looking in that corner and she couldn't image how she managed, but Cher was small.

"Hey Kay, where is your little Donna Karen purse? You know the blue one? Can I carry it tonight?" Teresa asked.

"Um, I let Cher use it a while ago, you should check her closet. I don't think she took it with her," Kennedy said, putting on her make-up.

Teresa ran down the steps and went into Cher's room. "Purse, purse, purse," Teresa said, looking around. She went into Cher's closet and wondered how she had so many clothes, shoes and purses and never had any money. She spotted the little blue purse but it was under a ton of other purses. She tried to pull it but ended up making about fifteen purses tumble down. "Damn," she said and began to pick them up. A plastic zip lock bag fell out of one of Cher's hand bags. Teresa picked it up to put it back into the bag, but she saw a picture that looked like Julian. She was curious, so she opened the bag and pulled out the picture. It looked like a picture of him and Kennedy, but Kennedy's face was marked out with black marker.

Teresa went through the bag and her mouth dropped. She didn't want to, but she took the bag upstairs. She turned the volume down on Kennedy's system and Kennedy stuck her head out the bathroom.

"What are you doing, girl? That is my song," she said bobbing her head to the music.

"Kennedy, come here and look at this," she said. Kennedy came out of the bathroom and Teresa sat on the bed.

"What is it?" she asked, confused.

"Sit down," Teresa said with the bag in her hand. "Now, when I give you this, I want you to know that I didn't go through Cher's stuff. It fell out of one of her handbags," she said, giving it to her. Kennedy flipped through the stuff and covered her mouth.

Chapter Twenty Four

'You know I love you and one day you and I will be as one. Please stop running and trying to fight the feelings because I know you want me, Julian. There is no way you want that fat bitch over me. If you gave me the chance, I can show you what real love is. I can please you better than she can, I know it, but you act like you don't want this. Julian, every man wants this and I'm offering it to you on a silver platter, but you keep bullshitting and if you keep this up I'm going make things so fucking bad for you and that bitch.'

Kennedy read and had to stop. She couldn't take it anymore. She went through the bag and there were so many pictures of her being marked out and letters. She imagined Cher never actually gave them to Julian unless she made a copy.

"I... I... I...," she stuttered because she was at a loss for words. She stood and began to pace. "That bitch!" she yelled and paced some more.

"Kennedy, come on sit down. Let me get you a drink."

"Ree, I don't want a drink. I want to beat the shit outta Cher," she said with anger in her eyes. She was so furious she, but didn't dare cry.

"Kennedy relax babe come on, calm down."

"I am calm Ree. I'm calm. I'm so fucking calm I could be on a patience billboard. I am calm. I am calm!" she yelled and went back into the bathroom to finish getting dress.

"Kennedy Renee what are you going to do?"

"What I should have done a long time ago Teresa Marie,"

she said, applying her eye shadow.

"What's that?"

"Get my man back and cut that bitch loose," she said and started smiling at her reflection in the mirror. She was a big girl, but she felt like she had dropped one hundred and twenty five pounds. She checked herself in the mirror in the foyer one more time and she and Teresa rode to the club.

Teresa was a little nervous because she thought Kennedy was acting too calm. She wondered if Cher's life was in danger, because Kennedy was just too cool.

They parked and Kennedy was not happy to see a white Lexus in the spot next to Julian Benz. That was where she normally parked, but she hadn't been there in over four months. When they got to the door, Greg the door man recognized them and was pleased to see Kennedy.

"Hey, Ms. Kennedy, Teresa, how are you ladies? Long time no see," he said, hugging the both of them.

"Hey Greg, it is good to see you," Kennedy said, excited to be back.

"Come on in, y'all know y'all are VIP. Does the boss know you're here?" he asked and reached for his walkie talkie.

"No and don't radio him. I want to surprise him," she said and winked.

"Al'righty then, you ladies have a good time," he said.

They went inside and scanned the room and didn't see him. She went over to the bar and Tony almost jumped over the bar when he saw her.

"Hey stranger, what's going on, girl?"

"Hey Tony, how are you?"

"I'm good, how you are?"

"Better," she said with a smile.

"Yeah your girl Cher stopped through here last night," he said, putting a wine glass in front of the both of them and poured them a drink.

"Yea, I heard," she said and tried to pay.

"You know your money is no good here," he said.

"I know Tony," she said and couldn't stop smiling. She was glad she decided to get there early to talk to Julian because there were not a lot of people there yet. "Hey Tony, where is he?" she asked. He pointed up to his office.

"I must warn you, he's not alone," he said, giving her the heads up.

"That's cool," she said and then Tony went over to service another customer. "Are you going to be cool for a little while by yourself?" she asked Teresa.

"Yep baby, I'm good. Go get your man back," she said.

Kennedy headed for the steps. She thought about Rona, but didn't care. It was either now or never she told herself and knocked.

"Yea," he yelled. She tapped again. "Come in," he said and she slowly opened the door. He was at his desk and Rona was sitting on the sofa sipping a drink and reading a magazine. Her mouth dropped when she saw Kennedy and Julian's heart stopped.

"Hello Julian," she said, smiling. "Hi Rona," she said, acknowledging her.

"Kennedy hey, I mean, come on in," he said, getting up. She was looking so beautiful and he wanted to hug her.

"I'm sorry to interrupt, but I need to talk to you," she said.

Rona tossed her magazine on the table and stood up. "I'm not leaving," she spat at Julian.

"Excuse me Kennedy," he said, moving closer to Rona. "Look, don't make a scene. Go downstairs and have a drink and give me a few moments."

"Hell no!" she yelled with her arms folded.

"You know what Rona, you're right. I will go and...," Kennedy tried to say.

"No Kennedy, hold on," Julian said, stopping her from leaving. Rona meant absolutely nothing to him and he wasn't about to put up with her fit. "Rona, I need to talk to Kennedy. Now, either you can go downstairs and give me a minute to talk to her or you can go downstairs, get in your car and leave, either way you are going to get out of my office so I can speak to her in private," he said. Even though Rona was young, she was not stupid. She got her purse and coat and rolled her eyes at Kennedy.

"Good bye, Julian," she said and he was fine with that.

"Good bye, Rona," he said and she headed for the door.

"Good bye, Rona," Kennedy said, making it clear that, that was good bye, not see you later.

"Good bye to you, Kennedy," she said and slammed his office door.

Julian turned to her. "Sorry about her," he said nervously.

"No need," she said, waving her hand toward the door.

"So, what's up?" he asked casually. She sat her drink down and took off her jacket and he took it and laid it on the chair.

"Can we sit?" she asked and got her glass. They went over to the sofa. She sat there and took a couple swallows of her drink before she spoke. "I know that it was Cherae," she said, looking straight ahead and not at him.

"Oh thank God," he said, able to breathe. He had no idea why she was there and he was hoping that his letter got through to her.

"Julian baby, I'm so sorry. I still can't believe it, but I know it's true that Cher did all the things you said she did."

"Baby, I'm sorry. I know that was hard for you," he said, reaching for her hand, and his touch felt good.

"It was so hard Julian, but I'm glad that I know. I am glad that it wasn't you. I miss you so much and I have never stop thinking about you. And I feel so foolish for just shutting you out."

"Don't, you did what you felt was the thing to do and it did look pretty bad," he said. She finished her drink and put the glass on the table next to Rona's unfinished martini.

"Julian, you said in your letter that you still loved me and if there was any chance for us to work it out, that's what you wanted to do," she said with her eyes welling. She swallowed hard and hoped he meant that.

"Yes," he said, moving closer to her.

"Was that true?" she asked and he kissed her tears on her cheek.

"Baby, I love you and I meant every word I wrote in that letter," he said, turning her to face him. "I have missed you so much Kennedy and I am overwhelmed right now that you are actually right here and I can do this," he said and kissed her deeply. Her nerves were waking up all over and his blood was rushing to his dick and in no time he had an erection.

"Aw baby, I want you so much," she said as he kissed her neck and rubbed her breast through her sweater. A tap on the door made them realize where they were.

"Yea," he said. Kennedy sat up and straightened her sweater and tried to wipe her eyes, but Rona came back in and when she saw them on the sofa like they were, she knew it was a bad scene.

"So that's it?" she asked, looking sad.

"Rona," he said, getting up. Kennedy knew she had to give him a minute to handle his business with her. She stood and grabbed her purse and headed for the door. "This will only take a few minutes," he told Kennedy.

"Okay," she said and gave him a smile.

"Don't leave I'll be down in a minute," he told her.

"I won't," she said and pulled the door up behind her.

She found Teresa and told her what happened and they went to the ladies room so she could fix her face. They went over to the table that was always reserved and of course it was available. They waited for Julian and Kennedy wondered what was keeping him. After a few moments, she saw Rona storm out of the door, so she figured that was done.

"Hey ladies," Julian said and sat next to Kennedy. He grabbed her hand to kiss it.

"Hey Julian, good to see you," Teresa said, smiling at him.

"Yea, it's good to see you as well," he said and turned back to Kennedy.

"So, that thing with Rona is done?" she asked and took a sip of her drink.

"Yes that's done," he said and leaned in to kiss her.

"Good," she said.

After dancing and drinking for a while, they could not keep their hands off each other. Kennedy gave Teresa the keys to her truck and she and Julian went back to her house.

Chapter Twenty Five

Kennedy was smiling 'til her mind went back to Cher. "That bitch came up here and got in my bed?" she said and Julian was caught off guard. They just finished making some serious good love and he didn't expect to hear her say that.

"Babe come on, I don't want to talk about her," he said, squeezing her tight. "I just want to enjoy you and bask in this after love making feeling," he said.

Kennedy was still angry. "I know, baby and I can't help it. I'm so pissed off about her ass I could kill her."

"Shhh baby, come here," he said, kissing her. "Don't get upset all over again please. I am so happy to have you in my arms again and your body feels so damn good right now. All I want to think about is us and getting some more of this good stuff right here," he said, touching her in her spot.

It was a good idea, but she wanted to tell him what she wanted to do the next day. "I know baby and this is so perfect. You felt so good to me and believe me I want some more, but I want to know what you got planned for tomorrow?"

"Well I was hoping to spend the entire day with you," he said and she smiled.

"Good, that is a very good idea, because we have work to do," she said and he was confused.

"Work baby, what are you talking about?" he asked, planting soft kiss on her shoulder.

"Well first thing in the morning, I'm going to get a storage and then I'm going to come home and pack all of her shit and put it out of my house. I'm also going to call a locksmith to come and change the damn locks," she said.

Julian didn't believe she was serious, but he was proud of her. "Okay baby that sounds great. Now can yo' man get some more?" he asked, rubbing her breast and squeezing her erect nipples.

"Oh yes, baby, you can get whatever you want," she said and let him penetrate her tunnel again. She closed her eyes and moaned like she was being injected with platinum. He felt so damn good and she knew that she wasn't going to let him go and the next bitch that tried that shit Cher tried was going to have to deal with her because she wasn't going anywhere.

The next morning, Kennedy was up early. She used Julian's car to go get the storage and got a few boxes from the storage place. She called her cousins and of course, they agreed to come over with a truck to haul all of Cher's stuff away. Teresa came over and was happy to see her friend in good spirits and going through with her plans to kick Cher out of her house and out of her life.

"Damn girl, Cher had a lot of shit," Teresa said.

"Yep, including pictures of Julian from my digital camera in her nightstand drawer," Kennedy said.

"You're lying," Teresa said.

"Nope, I guess I would have never actually believed it was her in my heart if you hadn't needed that purse last night."

"I guess not, so how do you feel?"

"I feel okay actually," she said, sweeping the floors. The room was finally empty and she was wondering what she was going to do with that space.

"Well I have some news for you," Teresa said.

"What, babe?" she asked, wondering how so much dust was on the floor.

"Well I didn't want to tell you last night because of all the drama that was going on, but Max proposed."

"Nooo…," Kennedy said, surprised.

"Yep on Thursday at dinner. Then you called about the

letter and I didn't want to bring it up," she said.

"That is great, Ree. Where's the ring?"

"It's right here," she said, going over to her purse that was hanging on the door handle. "It's too big and I don't want to take a chance of losing it," she said and showed it to Kennedy. "I'm going to get Jason to size it for me."

"Aw, it's beautiful Ree and he has excellent taste. Expensive taste," Kennedy said, examining it. It was top notch.

"Thank you girl. I've been putting it on every five minutes," she said, happy.

"I see why, it's beautiful. So, when is the wedding?"

"I don't know, we didn't talk about that yet," she said.

"I'm happy for you Ree," she said and hugged her and Julian walked in. "Hey baby, Ree's engaged," she announced.

"Wow Teresa, congratulations," he said, hugged her and kissed her on the cheek.

"Thanks," she said, still smiling.

"Look at her ring baby," Kennedy said.

"Aw, damn the brother got taste. He wasn't playing was he?" he joked and they laughed.

"Naw he wasn't," Kennedy commented as she went back to sweeping the floor. She was just about done.

"Baby, here's the key to the storage and Kory said if you need anything else let him know. And here are the new keys to the house," he said, handing them all to her.

"Thank you baby and here you go," she said handing him one of the copies. "You gotta keep a copy for yourself," she said with a smile and he gave her a quick kiss. "I'm glad y'all helped me because I'd still be in her with all the shit Cher had up in here."

"I know, I thought you had a lot of shoes, but damn," Julian said and they laughed.

"So, when is she coming back?"

"Tuesday I think," she said.

"Well look baby; I gotta head over to the club. Are you good?"

"Yea babe, I'm good. That's everything, so I'm good."

"I'm going to run by my house first to shower and change."

"Okay, I'll see you later," she said and he kissed her.

"Ree, are you coming tonight?"

"Naw, I'm staying in," she said.

"No, come on out, you and Maxwell. I'll have a table set up and we can celebrate the engagement."

"Okay, I'll call him," she said, going for her cell phone.

"Okay, I should see you by ten or so?" he asked Kennedy.

"Yeah, I should be there by then."

"Okay, I love you," he said and gave her another kiss.

"I love you too," she said and smiled brightly. He left and she and Ree went into the kitchen to eat the food he had picked up for them.

"Girl, it's so good to see you and Julian back together," Ree said and smiled.

"Thanks girl and it feels good too. I mean, so good."

"I bet," she said because she knew she meant the sex.

"Yes girl, last night, ooh chile. I'm so glad we are back together," she said and they slap five.

"So how you think girlfriend gon' act on Tuesday when she comes home?" Teresa asked and took a bite of her sandwich.

"Girl, I don't know and right now I don't even care," she said, picking the tomato off of her sandwich. Julian knew she was allergic, but since they had been apart for a spell she figured he forgot.

"Well I honestly think she is going to shit bricks," Teresa said and they laughed. Kennedy knew she was right, but she really didn't care because Cher had done the unthinkable to her and she no longer considered them to be friends.

They finished their meals and Kennedy walked Teresa to her car and thanked her again for helping her out that day. She went back inside and it was only seven, so she had a little while before she had to dress. She took her shower and decided to take a little nap.

Her ringing phone woke her up at ten after nine and when she saw it was Cherae, she didn't answer. She dressed and headed for the club and she was happy to see that Teresa and Max were already there. They all had a good time and when Kennedy and Julian got in they did the damn thing again. Kennedy was happy that everything went exactly the way it went because making up

was always so good.

Chapter Twenty Six

When Cher and Cortez pulled up, she smiled when she saw Julian's Benz parked in the driveway. She figured he took her advice and he and Kennedy were back together.

"Oh my God, they are back together…, yes," she said with excitement.

"That is Julian's Benz?" Cortez said as he parked.

"Yep, I knew she'd take him back," she said, anxious to get out. "No wonder why she hasn't answered her phone this entire weekend," she said. She just didn't know that Kennedy didn't have anything to say to her.

Cherae had such a good time with Cortez, she was only going home to grab some clothes and head back with him to his place. She was even actually thinking of settling down with him since she had such an awesome trip.

He was not Julian, but he was a good man. He was good looking and made good money. All the time she spent lusting over Julian, she had never really given Cortez a chance. Now all that was behind her she was ready to be right with Cortez and start a new relationship with her best friend. She had so many ideas going through her head about finally going to college and picking a career for herself. The talk with Kennedy and the trip with Cortez had Cher ready to start a new life.

"Are you going in with me?" she asked and undid her seatbelt.

"Yeah, I can holla at your friends," he said and they got out. It was cold and she couldn't wait to get inside. She put her key in the door and she tried to unlock it, but her key didn't work.

"What the hell?" she said and rang the doorbell. Kennedy came to the door and opened it. "Hey, hey," she said, smiling ear to ear. She was excited about Julian being there and she was expecting Kennedy to be bursting with excitement. "I see y'all made up and are back together."

"Yeah, thanks to you," Kennedy said with a smile.

"So, he took my advice and called you?" she said, then remembered her key not working. "And what's going on with the door? My key wouldn't work," she said, taking off her coat and Cortez shut the door. Julian stood there and they were all in the foyer. "Hey Julian, I told you to just call," Cherae said and winked at him. "Man, its cold outside," Cher said and then realized something was wrong because Kennedy was damn near blocking her path. "Hey, what's going on?" she asked, feeling awkward.

"Here is your new key," Kennedy said, giving her the key to the storage.

"Oh, thanks. What happened? Why did we get new locks?" she asked, confused. She hoped nothing terrible happened while she was gone and the reason why Julian was really there because Kennedy was afraid to be alone. The look of confusion on her face quickly changed to worry. "Are you okay, Kennedy? Did someone try to break into the house?" she asked seriously.

"Well we no longer live together and we are no longer friends Cher," she said.

Cher was confused. "What..., what are you talking about, Kay?" she asked, wondering what in the hell happened. "What in the hell did you tell her Julian?" she yelled.

"Everything," he said, telling the truth. Kennedy's plan was to see if she was going to tell her the truth.

"You bastard, I asked you to go back to Kennedy because I knew you guys had a chance, not for you to lie your way back in," she snapped.

"What did I lie about Cher?" he asked her with his arms folded, waiting for her to answer.

"Yes Cher, since you think Julian is here because he lied, what could he have lied about?"

"Kennedy, I don't know what this asshole told you or what he tried to brainwash you with, but I'm sure he made up something," she snapped.

"Well baby, why don't you tell Cher exactly what you told me to see if your story matches her story," Kennedy said.

"Okay babe, let's see. I told you about the night when you were at Ree's when she crept into your bed and gave me head and about the morning when you came home because you forgot your phone, how she hid behind the chair in your room. Um, let's see, I told you why I put the lock on my office door because Cher used to barge in there whenever she felt like it and take off her clothes and you know the rest," he said.

Cher was furious. She didn't believe her ears and more important, he said everything right in front of Cortez. "You are a motherfucking liar, Julian. You don't actually believe any of this bullshit, do you Kennedy?" she asked, looking at Kennedy like she was afraid to death.

"You know something Cher, I didn't believe him. I really thought that he was out of his mind. I told Julian to lay off the Crown because it was fucking up his head for him to say those horrible things about my best friend. He musta been on some type of crack, not Cher, not my sister, is what I told him and then you know what I did, Cherae Monique? I cried my eyes out. I just knew Cher would never ever do any of those awful things to me. I took a day off and told myself to forget about Julian and move on with my life.

"Cherae, I went shopping, to the spa and decided I'd go out to have a little fun and maybe I'd meet a new man," she said, stretching the truth. "Teresa and I were getting ready to go out and she asked me about my little blue Donna Karen purse. You know, the one I let you borrow a few months ago, that you never returned?

"Yes, you know the one, so I sent her downstairs to your room and she looked through your closet for it and guess what?" she asked. Cherae almost fainted. She already knew what she had in her closet buried in one of her purses. "You know what she found amongst your purses?" Kennedy asked and went over to the coffee table and got the zip lock bag.

"Now, before you say a word, Cherae Monique, because I know you know what I'm holding, tell me why? I've been your friend since we were seven and this is what you think of me Cher?" she asked. Cher was speechless. She knew there was plenty of evilness in that bag and she couldn't lie, nor could she speak. "Answer me, dammit!" Kennedy yelled.

"I need my things," she said and brushed by Kennedy. Kennedy didn't stop her, because she wanted her to see just how for real she was. She stood there and waited for Cher's reaction.

"Kay!" she yelled from her empty room and she stomped back to the foyer. "What did you do with my stuff?"

"That key that I gave you is to your storage. Here is their card," Kennedy said. "Unit 41, it's paid up for six months and after that, you are on your own."

"Kay, you can't be serious," she said, mustering up a few tears.

"Cher, I am so serious this time. You have used, abused and back stabbed me for the last time."

"Kennedy, please…," she cried.

"Kennedy, please what, Cher?"

"I'm begging you…," she said, pleading.

"Aren't you tired of begging me Cher? I don't owe you anything right now but an ass whippin' and if it weren't for the fact that it is the dead of winter, I'd take your ass outside," she said and Julian chuckled.

"Kennedy, can we go in the other room please, so just you and I can talk?" she said, crying.

"No, you cannot sweet talk me or pull one of your moves on me. I am done with you and I never want to see you or talk to you ever again."

"Kay you don't mean that, we can get past this. I'm so sorry for everything. You are right, I am a liar and I have been a terrible friend. I went after your man and I lied about everything because I was a selfish, jealous bitch and I'm so sorry, please don't do this," she begged.

"Yes you are and now please Cher, just go," she said, not able to look at her.

"Kay, I love you so much, please, please, you are the only family I have," she said, trying to grab Kennedy's hand and Kennedy snatched away.

"No, no, no, Cher, stop it, okay. Stop it!" she yelled. She was hurt and so upset and it was difficult for Kennedy to treat Cherae that way, but it had to be done.

"Kay, I'm so sorry for everything. I'll go, but please don't end our friendship, please. I'm begging you, I love you so much and I know I hurt you."

"Cher, I love you too," she said and hugged her real tight. "This is killing me Cher, it really is, but I got to say goodbye to you," she said. Cher couldn't believe she was for real. She released her embrace and walked away. She went upstairs to keep from saying another word to Cher.

"Listen Cortez, I'm sorry you had to witness this," Julian said.

"It's cool," he said. "Cher baby, come on," he said, trying to grab her hand.

"No!" Cherae yelled. "I need to talk to Kay," she said, going to the bottom of the steps. "Kennedy Renee, I'm sorry, I'm sorry, Kennedy please, I'm sorry," she said, crying. Cortez came and pulled her to the door. "Are you happy now?" she yelled at Julian. "You see what you've done?" she yelled, crying.

"Cher you did this, not me. How can you say you're sorry and still blame me?"

"You turned her against me," she cried.

"Cher baby come on," Cortez said, pulling her arm. Julian opened the door. "Cher," he said pulling her. She finally gave in and walked out. Julian closed the door and ran up the steps to check on Kennedy.

"Baby, are you okay?" he asked.

"Jay please babe, I don't want to talk right now," she said, sobbing.

"Okay baby, I'll be downstairs if you need me," he said and paused before he left. "Kennedy, I'm so proud of you. You can't see it now, but you did the right thing."

"If I did the right thing Jay, why do I feel so horrible?" she asked. He came in and he sat on the bed.

"Well babe, I can't answer that. Do you remember when we broke up and you felt that if I would do something so horrible to you, even though you loved me, the best thing was to let me go?"

"Yeah," she said, sniffling.

"Well Cher did some bad things to you and even though you love her, you don't need what she gives you in your life. So, the best thing for you was to rid yourself of her because she wasn't good for you. Cher wasn't your friend, babe."

"I know that, but it's like losing a family member. I know she has issues, but I am going to miss her."

"Baby its hard now, but it will get easier. It's just going to take some time," he said and it did.

Chapter Twenty Seven

"So where do you want to go?" Cortez asked Cher as he cranked the engine. He was upset and angry as hell and she wasn't about to go home with him.

"What do you mean?" Cher asked.

He wondered was she really as clueless as she was acting, because she was acting as if he just did not hear how she had been trying to fuck another man while they had been together. "What do you mean, 'what do I mean'? You're kidding me right? Now where would you like for me to take you?" he asked in a very serious tone.

"Cortez, what do you mean? I don't have anywhere else to go," she cried.

"Well you should have thought of that before you tried to sleep with your best friend's man."

"Cortez please, baby, I don't have anywhere to go. You just can't leave me out in the cold."

"Oh sweetie, trust you are not going home with me. We've been together just as long as Kennedy and Julian, so that means you weren't thinking of me and our relationship if you wanted Julian so much. That's why you kept pulling back and pushing me away when I wanted more. I see now where your head is."

"Cortez please, that was before. I've changed and I tried to get them back together before our trip. That was months ago Cortez and the trip you and I just had made us so much closer. Baby I'm not trying to ruin what I have with you, so please, let's just go to your place and talk about it," she suggested. He wasn't interested in that idea.

"No, that is not what's going to happen and you not having anywhere to go is not my problem. Now, I can drop you where ever you want to go, but you are not going to my place."

"Cortez, what am I supposed to do, huh? Where can I go?" she asked, looking at him teary eyed.

"I can get you to a hotel and then you can get yourself some help," he suggested, because apparently she was off to think he would just let what he just heard go.

"Cortez please, I can't afford a hotel," she said, looking at him like he was insane.

"That's your problem, not mine," he said and continued to drive. He didn't know where she wanted to go, but he kept driving.

"Okay then fine, just take me to your place to get my car," she said with an attitude.

"Oh, that's cool," he said, mad as hell and didn't give a damn that she had an attitude. When he got to his house he pulled into the garage and got out. He didn't bother to invite her in and he locked his door right behind him once he got inside. She got in her car and cranked the engine to let it warm up. She had no idea where she was going to go, so she sat there and cried for an hour.

She got out and banged on Cortez's door for ten minutes, demanding that he help her, but he didn't let her in and he threatened to call the cops if she didn't go away. She got back into her car and she thanked God it was warm. She took out her cell phone and called four of her ex boyfriends and none of them wanted to see her or help her out. She took a huge chance and drove to Teresa's and when Teresa opened the door she shook her head.

"You have got to be kidding me Cher. Why are you here? Why would you think for one second that it would be okay to come here?" she asked, standing in the doorway. It was cold as hell, but Teresa declared Cher was not coming into her house.

"Ree, come on, please? Kennedy kicked me out. I have no place to go. Can I please stay here for a night or two?"

"Look Cher, you cannot stay here and I don't feel sorry for you because you did a number on Kennedy. I'm not Kennedy baby and you will not use me and you are not going to talk me into allowing you to crash at my house."

"Okay, okay, Ree just for tonight. One night 'til I figure out what to do."

"No, Max is here and with your track record, I don't trust your trifling ass, goodnight," Ree said and shut the door in Cher's face.

Cher stood there in disbelief for a few moments, but it was cold so she hurried to get back into her car. Teresa went straight for the phone to tell Kennedy that Cher tried to stay at her place and Kennedy wasn't surprised.

Cher sat in her car and the tears burned her eyes. She only had a few dollars and it wasn't enough to get a room for the night. Her cards were maxed out and she didn't have any other girlfriends. All of her co-workers hated her because she was prettier than they all were, at least that's what Cher thought, but it was because Cher was a conceited bitch and they hated to be around her stuck up ass. After sitting and thinking, she headed for the club. She didn't know why, but she knew she could sit at the bar at least 'til four and then maybe stay in her car 'til it was early enough to go to work.

She figured she'd go by the gym so she could shower and brush her teeth and would see what guy at her job she could sob to and maybe convince one of them to put her up for a few days. She sat at the bar and Tony came over to greet her. He didn't have to ask what she was having because he knew what she liked.

"Damn Cher, why the long face? It looks as if you've lost your best friend. I have never seen you looking like this girl. What in the hell?" he asked, pushing the Coke button, adding Coke to her drink.

"Yeah, I did something awful and I lost my best friend," she said and took a huge gulp of her drink. She hoped Tony would put it on the house like he usually did.

"Damn girl, what happened?"

"Well you remember last year right before Kennedy and Julian got together we asked you to draw a card?"

"Oh yea, when Jay first brought this place," he said, recalling that night.

"Yea well, I tried to fuck him and I fucked myself," she said, being honest. She told him the entire story play by play.

159

"Now I don't have a place to go," she said, crying and drinking her fourth Hennessy and Coke that she wasn't paying for because Tony kept them coming.

"Damn girl, whatcha gon' do?"

"Hell Tony, I don't know. I don't get paid 'til Friday and I don't know," she said, sobbing.

"Well I got a futon," he offered, feeling sorry for her. "But, you gotta go by Friday. My girl is a flight attendant and she will be home Friday evening."

"You and that chick that I seen you with live together?"

"No, but she'd kill my ass if she saw you at my crib. Even if it is innocent, she wouldn't believe that in a million years," he said.

She laughed a little because she knew he was right. Most women felt intimidated around her and didn't want their man to be anywhere alone or near her without being present. She sat there grateful that Tony offered her a place to lay her head for a couple nights. She waited 'til they closed and was so sleepy by the time they made it to his place.

She was relieved that his place was nice and clean. She took a long shower and decided she'd take a sick day the next day so she could get her mind right. She was messed up and didn't know where she'd begin to get her life back on track. She was sorry for what she had done to Kennedy and had to tell herself that she was not sorry for putting herself in an "ass out situation," but she was sorry for betraying the only friend that she had. She knew that it was not going to be an easy fix, but she was definitely determined to make amends with Kennedy.

She felt bad for Cortez and wished she hadn't taken him for granted for all those months and she didn't know if she and he would ever have another chance. She honestly had fallen for him and she knew how bad Kennedy and Julian had to feel when she broke them up because she would have rather been in bed with Cortez instead of lying in Tony's spare bedroom on a futon. She let the tears fall and wished again that she was not an evil bitch. She prayed and asked God to forgive her and to help her get her life on track.

The next couple of days dragged as she made a thousand

attempts to talk to Kennedy while Kennedy ignored her. She tried and tried to talk to Cortez, but he ignored her as well and she was all alone in her little overpriced roach motel. She was glad the heat worked because that was all she could afford. Tony allowed her to come back and forth while his girlfriend was out of town.

After the first month, Cortez was still avoiding her and Cher was miserable. She cried day in and day out and begged God to help her. She followed Kennedy around, went by the store and Kennedy had to threatened her with a restraining order to keep her from showing up every day. She didn't stop calling her and Kennedy never did pick up. She continued to pursue Cortez and was still getting nowhere.

After three months, he finally took her back and let her move in with him because she was penniless. She and Cortez made every attempt to work it out because he loved her and when she'd bring up Kennedy he would tell her to just let it go.

After a while of unanswered letters, phone calls and emails, Cher settled with the fact that she had damaged the best thing she ever had. It was hard, but she decided to just move on without Kennedy.

Chapter Twenty Eight

It was spring and Kennedy hadn't talked to Cher and she avoided her at all cost. Cher called her every day for five months and she finally stopped. She'd come to the club and Kennedy would ignore her like she wasn't there. She'd come over to Kennedy's table or to the bar where she sat and Kennedy would not look at her. It was hard, but she did it.

By the summer, Kennedy and Julian were inseparable. He opened another club and it was like Kennedy was his partner because besides working the door, she had learned how to fix drinks and spin a couple of records if she had to. A year had gone by and Maxwell and Teresa were married and she was having her first baby at thirty six. Kennedy and Julian were still a power team, working side by side, making things happen. Business was busy, but together they held it down.

Teresa was the general manager of the jewelry store and Kennedy was all over the place. The restaurants, the clubs and the store and she stayed busy, but she enjoyed every moment of it because she got to work alongside her man. She couldn't help but love her life, but she still thought of Cherae from time to time and wondered how she was.

"Hey," Teresa said to Kennedy when she walked into the jewelry store.

"Hey, how is the mommy to be?"

"Sick as usual," she replied.

"Aw, I'm sorry, baby. It'll get better soon. I'm sure it will."

"Shit, when? I'm already four months and if I throw up one

more time, I swear she is going come out of my mouth."

"She?" Kennedy asked.

"Just hoping, we already have a son," she said, talking about her husband's son.

"Well good luck," she said and came around the counter.

"Thanks. Oh, it's a package on your desk," Teresa said.

"Okay, but I wasn't expecting any shipments 'til Monday," she said, wondering if there was a mix up.

"Well one came in this morning," she said.

Kennedy went into her office. The package on her desk didn't look like a normal delivery from the factory. It was a pretty pink package with a bow. She sat at her desk and opened it. It was a card that read, '*You are the best thing that ever happened to me." Kennedy Renee Banks, will you make me the happiest man in the world by being my wife?*' She read it and put the card down and another box was inside the box she opened.

She opened it and it was a black, velvet ring box. She opened it and her eyes lit up when she saw the diamond. She recognized the cut and knew her daddy had to definitely be in on that one. She was occupied with the package she didn't notice everyone piling into the store on the monitors. She grabbed the box and ran to the front and everybody was there.

"Surprise!" everyone yelled. She was blown away. Her daddy, her uncles, her cousins, her staff and Julian's staff from the clubs and the restaurants were packed into her store and she wondered how they all came in so fast. She was holding her chest because they scared the shit out of her when she opened the door to go back to the front.

"Oh my God! What in the hell are you guys trying to do, give me a heart attack?" she asked, holding her chest.

"No baby that is not what we were trying to do. Well they may have, but I'm trying to make you my wife," he said and everyone laughed. He moved closer to her and took the box from her hand. He took the ring out and slid it on her finger, even though she never said yes. "So, what's it going be?" he asked.

"Well this ring is beautiful and you are sorta good looking, so, umm..., I guess I will," she said. They kissed and everybody applauded. She wanted to dance and celebrate and still wished

Cherae was in her life to share her happiness.

Chapter Twenty Nine

"Baby, can you host for about fifteen minutes to let Kelley go on break?" Julian asked his wife because she was in the office doing the payroll.

"Yeah baby, give me one minute to save this," she said, saving her work.

They were newlyweds and when they got home from their honeymoon it was back to work. They were at one of the restaurants and they were doing what they were accustomed to doing; working hard, playing hard and loving each other hard. Life was good and things were good and Kennedy didn't have one reason to complain.

Kennedy took the clipboard from Kelley and let her go on break. They alerted Kennedy that a table in the non smoking section was available and she called the next name.

"Brooks, party of two," she called. She almost fainted when she saw Cherae and Cortez. She was beautiful as ever, had a ring on her finger and a baby in her womb. She was pregnant and even more beautiful than the last time Kennedy saw her. "Cher," Kennedy said, overjoyed to see her.

"Oh my God, Kay," she said. They hugged and each other tight for a while. They finally let go and Kennedy touched her face and they hugged again. Forgetting all the pain and the anguish she went through with her.

"You work here?" Cher asked, wondering why she was hosting at a restaurant.

"Yes, I mean, no…, I mean, we own this place. Julian and I

were married about three weeks ago," she said excited and held up her hand to show off her gorgeous ring.

"Wow, your ring is lovely. Of course, you remember Cortez and we are married and as you can see, we are expecting," she said, showing off her ring. Hers was gorgeous as well.

"I see," Kennedy said, trying to hold back the tears. "Come on follow me," she said and got them to their table because spectators were all up in their reunion. She seated them, gave the clipboard to another employee and went to find Julian.

"Baby, you will never believe who is here," she said excited.

"Who baby, Michael Jordan?" he asked, joking.

"Cher baby…, Cher and Cortez."

"Cher," he said, not pleasantly surprised.

"Yes, you have to come see her baby, she is so beautiful and she is pregnant Jay. You got to come see. She and Cortez are married, come on baby," she said pulling his arm.

"Cher as in Cherae?" he said, resisting. He wasn't excited.

"Yes Cher, come on," she said, pulling him.

"Hold up baby," he said, bringing her back to reality. "Baby, this is Cher," he said again.

"I know baby, but that was so long ago and I'm done with grudges and shit. So, come on, come baby, come say hello. Cortez is here, too," she said and Julian followed.

They ended up sitting down with them and they talked for hours. Kennedy filled her in on the events that transpired since they stop talking and how she sold her gorgeous home and Julian's bachelor's pad and brought their new home together. She told her how Teresa had a little girl and was pregnant again and how she and Julian were trying. When it was time to leave, Kennedy and Cher walked ahead the guys.

"Look Cher, I'm so happy to see you and I'm so happy to see that you are doing so well. I have always wanted the best for you and I'm glad that you are happy."

"Girl, Cortez is heaven sent. I am a real estate agent now because of him and our new company is booming, but this little one trying to slow me down, but we got it. I work from home mostly and it's been a change," Cherae said, sounding so much more mature and like the woman Kennedy knew she had it in her to be.

"That's good, Cherae Monique, that's so good," she said, holding her hands.

"Look, Kennedy, you were an awesome friend to me and I know I did some horrible…," she tried to say

"Cherae, you don't have to," she said, stopping her from reliving the pass.

"No Kay, this has to be said, okay. I'm glad you did what you did. I deserved everything I got for all the damage I did. I treated the most important person in my life so wrong and when you kicked me out, you helped me to change my life. You did so much for me and I depended on you for everything and I was in this state of mind that you were going to fall in love and move on without me and I did something terrible and I'm sorry. You were my sister Kennedy and I was a rotten friend. When you put me out I had to get my life together because Cortez wasn't having it, you hear me.

"No tantrums, no pouting, no whining, or slacking and if I was going to be with him I had to do my share and that was so new to me because you and your family has taken care of me since we were kids. Men did whatever I wanted them to do and I didn't know how to give back. Now I'm stronger and I know now what you have been telling me for years. I got to work for what I need and not depend on anyone and I get it now. It took me maybe too long, but I get it," she said and Kennedy smiled.

"Aw, Cherae Monique, I'm so happy for you, truly I am. I think of you all the time and I'm glad you finally got your shit together," she said and they laughed.

"I love you, Kennedy Renee and you will always be my best friend," she said.

"I love you too, Cherae Monique and you are still my best friend," she said and hugged her tight.

They exchanged numbers and took it one day at a time. Cherae had a baby boy and asked Kennedy and Julian to be the Godparents. Teresa had another girl and decided to tie her tubes. Julian and Kennedy finally got pregnant after one year of trying and were blessed with twins. Kennedy knew that was God's way of giving her what they needed because at thirty eight, she was in no position to have anymore.

The End

Book Club Questions

1. Do you think Cherae should have told Kennedy the night that they met Julian that she was interested.
2. Do you think Kennedy was too naïve?
3. Do you think it would have made a difference if Julian would have told Kennedy the truth the first time Cherae hit on him?
4. Do you think Kennedy was wrong for forgiving Cherae and not forgiving Julian the first time?
5. Do you think Cortez was crazy for forgiving Cherae?
6. Do you think Julian should have not taken Kennedy back for not believing him when he told her the truth?
7. Do you think Kennedy should have kept her relationship with Cherae buried after seeing her later on?
8. Do you feel that Kennedy should have not forgiven Cherae
9. Do you think Cherae honestly changed?
10. Do you think Cherae and Kennedy's friendship can be solid again after everything that happened?

About the Author

ANNA BLACK is a native of Chicago, but now resides in Texas with her husband and daughter. **Luck of the Draw** is her second published fiction novel and she will soon release her third novel, **Who Can I Run To**. She is a fulltime writer and she loves taking care of her family..

She would love to hear from her readers and supporters, so please feel free to contact her at the following:

www.annablack.net
annablackreaders@ymail.com
www.delphinepublications.com

FELISHABRADSHAW

DELPHINE PUBLICATIONS presents

EYES ON THE PRYZE

CPSIA information can be obtained at www.ICGtesting.com
Printed in the USA
LVOW051753140612

286160LV00004B/70/P